Helena Paneyko

THE MARKED PREY

Why They Were Targeted

Helena Paneyko

Translated from Spanish
By Keith Guerin

HELENA PANEYKO

Copyright January 2025 Helena Paneyko

All rights reserved. This book or any portion thereof may not be reprinted or used in any manner whatsoever without the express written permission of the publisher except for the use of brief quotation in a book review or scholarly journal.

This novel is a work of fiction, and any resemblance to reality with which someone may identify is simply coincidental.

First Printing: January 2025

ISBN: 9798306800073

Published by:
The Voice of Spanish
helenapaneyko@gmail.com

THE MARKED PREY

Table of Contents

DEDICATION	v
PROLOGUE	vi
MY STORY BEGINS HERE	1
A LITTLE HISTORY	5
THE MISSION	9
ANOTHER TYPE OF MEETING	11
FORTITUDE, HEART	15
IF YOU BELIEVE IT, YOU CREATE IT	18
THE PIECES OF THE PUZZLE	21
THE HANGOVER	26
DELEGATING IS THE KEY	28
AND MY SPECIAL GUESTS	33
THE MEETING WITH THE NURSE	35
MARIELA'S SECRETS	37
WHEN I CAME HOME	41
I HAD TO FIND	44
THE CASE OF THE BABY AS A DISTRACTION	46
THEY KEPT COMING	49
THE CALL OF ORLANDO	50
ALL SAINTS DAY	55
MARIELA	57
TWO WEEKS LATER	59
RAMIRO	60
PRIVATE INVESTIGATIONS	62
GUADALUPE RETURNED	64
A NEW CALL	66
IT WAS STILL DAYLIGHT	68
ASSIMILATING	72
THE FIRST SELECTION	73
A REVELATION	76
PREPARING FOR CHRISTMAS	78
FINALLY, THE HOOD IS REMOVED	80
PART TWO	81
MY GOD, WHERE AM I?	82
THE PAPERS	85
THE MIRROR	88

THE NEW PLAN	92
THE UNEXPECTED NEWS	96
TRAPPED WITH NO WAY OUT	98
THE IMMIGRANT'S MANUAL	100
A FEW MONTHS HAVE PASSED	102
TOTAL PARANOIA	106
DON'T EVEN THINK ABOUT IT	109
KIANA	112
COULD I COME OUT OF MY HIDING PLACE NOW?	114
MY FIRST CASE	119
PRUDENT SOUL	123
THANKSGIVING WAS APPROACHING	126
MORE CASES WERE OPENED	128
REFERENCE	130
MAP OF CRIMES USING ARTIFICIAL INTELLIGENCE	132
ACKNOWLEDGEMENTS	133
ABOUT THE AUTHOR	134
OTHER BOOKS BY THE AUTHOR	136
ABOUT THE TRANSLATOR	138

DEDICATION

I want to dedicate this novel to all those who have had to endure the anguish and hardships of having to leave their homelands and who have not let themselves be overwhelmed by the difficulties.

To all those who continue to excel in foreign lands.

To those who are grateful to those who have extended their hand to us and adopted us in their countries without having to do so.

PROLOGUE

One day I asked myself, And now that I'm here, what can I do for those who haven't been able to come?

Emigrating is a very hard and difficult journey.

The decision to leave behind the country where you were born, where you grew up, where you were educated and worked, where you have your family, your friends and your roots, where you dreamed and built, where the sound of the drums and the rhythm of salsa have moved your feet and your body for as long as you can remember, and the waves of the Caribbean Sea crash hard on the rocks leaving the smell of salt water in the air, where the desert covers you with sand that flies with the wind, and the snow envelops the Andes mountains with its mantle, where the sound of the macaws in the capital awakens your enthusiasm when you see them fly, and you enjoy the colorful herons and the oasis in the middle of the plains, where the wild waters of the southern rivers make you tremble with emotion full of porpoises playing innocently, where there is so much human warmth and home. Who in their right mind wants to leave there? There are circumstances that force you to make that decision. It's when you are drowned by the bloody hands of those in power and you can't breathe anymore, it's when you can't speak because they will silence you without compassion, and it's when you have no breath left or tears to dry.

So I decided to write about the other side of the immigrant story.

And I read, I studied, I researched, I asked questions, and I threw myself at the keyboard. Each word I wrote made me relive my experiences and those of many others. When I sat down in front of the computer, it was as if I were transported to each of the images I describe and the actions I narrate.

Life sometimes puts us in challenging situations and challenges us in ways we never imagined. Every day was different, unpredictable. We had become pieces of fate to be negotiated with. I learned to think, evaluate and act behind the facade of Doña Santa, the nickname I had earned within the community. Resilience and the ability to adapt to adversity are incredibly powerful. The genes of my ancestors, forged in misfortunes and dreams, had prepared me for the unthinkable and I was no longer frightened or surprised by the heartbreaking stories about the inhuman experiences of those who had to emigrate. The nauseating smells of blood, excrement, tears, and palpable fear were mixed with the hope that they would be in the past. The illusion of leaving those horrors behind was the powerful force to be able to continue. But will it be possible to leave all that behind?

I cannot turn my back on the unfortunate lives of those who have had to leave so much and everything behind, to start over somewhere else, with their dignity broken, their souls indignant, and with an uncertain future.

Alma

THE MARKED PREY

MY STORY BEGINS HERE

Finally it was time to rest after a long day filled with ambitious projects to complete that, instead of diminishing once completed, increased as if they were infinite, as if they were dreams. I always had something to do, something to think about, something to solve. My list of ideas kept getting fuller and fuller. As I laid my head on the pillow I tried to turn over in bed, careful not to wake my husband, whose snoring was so loud that it seemed even the neighbors could hear it. I think he imagined he was a racing motorcycle. I had already gotten used to those noises, now I barely noticed them.

The nightmares drenched me in sweat. They could have been signs of menopause, but at such a young age, that seemed unlikely. Ramiro, ignorant of female biology, did not question my explanations. In reality, he had no idea about my changes, but he accepted the simple and convincing scientific excuses I invented for him. They also served as a pretext for avoiding him. I knew, however, that it was something else. I had to endure and keep quiet.

After completing my revalidation exam and being accepted into the Mexican Veterinary Association, I decided to open my own animal hospital, treating animals from the smallest to the largest. I felt that I connected with them and with their tremors caused by the fear they felt when they came to my office. I confess that I also tremble inside when I have to go to the doctor or the dentist. I spoke to the animals calmly and without rushing, inspiring confidence in them. Once I saw that they were calmer, I explained to them what was happening to them and what I was going to do to them. Of course, I also listened to their owners, who gave me some clues, although sometimes they made up some stories that were a little hard to believe. It seemed that my method worked, not with all quadrupeds and some on two legs, but with most of them. The most reluctant would be convinced with other less pleasant methods.

My husband didn't like me to work, but I'm not one to stay home and do housework, and I made that clear from the beginning of our relationship.

I began my professional practice modestly in the garage of our residence: an examination table, a stethoscope, surgical supplies, a small refrigerator for vaccines and other products, and a second-hand microscope in very good condition. I think the local people liked me. When they came to my office, I always treated them with great respect and tried to help them with the knowledge and experience accumulated over the years. If I didn't have a logical answer, I dared to create hypotheses, researching without giving up until I found it.

To expand the services for animals, I decided to open a dog training school. This school offered various specialties, from a police dog academy with modalities such as search and rescue, drug detectors, cadaver search, and guard and custody, to animal training for people with disabilities of all kinds and even for programs to help children with reading. The school hired highly qualified trainers for these services and our trained animals began to be in demand not only in Mexico, but internationally.

That Thursday, however, began a nightmare that would not let me rest in peace. Miguel González brought his spectacular German Shepherd to the appointment, imported from Germany a few years ago and trained in the noble and difficult task of detecting drugs. Benito, recognized as one of the K9s with the best instincts and most experience in the Tepalcatepec Police Department (Michoacán, MX), had health problems atypical for the area. I took his blood for analysis and, to my surprise, I found a mutation of a trypanosome, a protozoan that affects both some mammals and humans in tropical areas. But how had it gotten into the blood of Benito, Miguel González's dog? I had to leave him hospitalized and under observation while I treated him. I couldn't predict the prognosis at that time.

My investigation had to focus not only on the parasite, which looked similar but was not the typical one I was used to, but also on finding out where and what it had been involved in to become infected. The next day, on Friday, another dog arrived who had graduated from our academy years before. In this case it was Bruno, trained to find corpses. He had the same symptoms as Benito, and coincidentally, the same trypanosome. In addition to the new trypanosome mutant, very similar but with some differences from the original, we found something else in common. Inside the stool there was a small and strange metal device.

Things were starting to smell fishy. I kept asking myself questions and questions. I began to piece together my puzzle by listening to comments from other colleagues who were also worried, curious and scared… Scared?

A LITTLE HISTORY

In Puerto Escondido, in the state of Oaxaca, in southern Mexico, I met the man who would become my future husband. I had always imagined him to be someone tall and thin, intelligent, cultured, and with a sophisticated last name. As they say, one proposes and God disposes.

I had gone to spend a few days with some friends from Caracas, my hometown. We had been told that it was a fabulous place to surf, and we enthusiastically confirmed this by using some boards rented from one of the kiosks on Carrizalillo beach. The waves were spectacular.

From the shore, a group of admirers watched our daring stunts in amazement. Among them was the man who would become my future husband. He approached the group and introduced himself: "Ramiro Ramirez, at your service," he said.

At first, he seemed a bit bold and heavy for my taste. His compliments were too much, and I had to stop him without discretion, without filter, and without compassion. That took him by surprise. He was used to submissive and helpful women who don't dare to say what they think, but I'm not like that. I had never imagined having a partner as ugly and ordinary as him. I think that, in addition to my athletic abilities and my personality, he was taken out of his comfort zone and began to seek me out, to invite me, and to make me fall in love.

Ramiro, whom I nicknamed the sinister dwarf, invited us all to his house in Morelia, Michoacán, with all expenses paid. I knew our vacation was about to end. We accepted. There we went and ended up staying in a very well-known five-star hotel, The five childhood friends. A star for each of us. We knew each other from school and from the Beach Club, where we shared almost every weekend for many years, from when we were children until each of us left for university.

The fact that Venezuelan women were known to be among the most beautiful in the world, as well as having a cheerful and lively personality, quickly made us a very popular group that everyone wanted to meet, entertain and invite to their parties and feasts.

On July 25th, during the Santiago Apóstol festival, known as Capula, Ramiro asked the band that was livening up the place for the microphone, and in front of the crowd he proposed to me. What a shame! I turned red as a tomato. How had this fat little guy thought of putting me in that situation in front of so many people? I think he took advantage of the fact that I was a little drunk, and I said yes. When the effects of the drinks wore off, I realized the mistake I had made, but it was too late to turn back. I was, and am, a woman of my word and I face the consequences with grace and sanity, whenever possible.

A few months later we got married in the Metropolitan Cathedral of Morelia.

It was a very beautiful wedding, broadcast on local television, since Ramiro was a well-known politician, a candidate for governor. This also helped him win votes among the citizens. He spared no expense. My dress was designed by Randy F., who became very famous after our marriage. There were fireworks, mariachis and food for everyone. That wedding would be remembered as the event that marked history, not only for Michoacán, but also for each one of us. And yes, up until that moment, Ramiro had behaved like a gentleman with me. Every week he brought me flowers and indulged me with any whim that occurred to me. I, however, always remained a little discreet and was not as affectionate as he was, he did not inspire bad thoughts in me, and he accepted his role as a devoted husband. He made up for it with scandalous outings and very well accompanied. Those nights, thank God, he did not return home and I could sleep peacefully. I did not ask anything. Why would I? Would anything change?

The initial fervor of falling in love was beginning to fade. I had gotten married in church and felt obliged to keep my marriage "intact" and follow the social norms of living together. I felt as if I was building my own prison without having the courage to stop it. I began to isolate myself emotionally. Although I was surrounded by people and not facing financial problems, I felt more alone than ever, I felt invisible. I learned to pick my battles, letting Ramiro believe he always won. This fed his macho ego, deeply rooted in our culture. Our marriage was changing. It was crumbling into little pieces, like cookies when you squeeze them too hard.

THE MISSION

My husband won the state governorship, and we moved into a mansion specially built for the family of the current governor. That house resembled, in size, the White House of the United States, but in the Spanish colonial style. The property occupied two complete blocks. It had rooms for meals, dances, and press conferences, a movie theater, a fabulous pool, very comfortable rooms, each with its own private bathroom. The internal corridors led to gardens with exotic plants, ferns, and large, colorful flowers, including bromeliads, orchids, sunflowers, roses, and birds of paradise; in short, a great variety of plants that attracted a great number of little birds that cheered us with their songs. The bees also seemed happy with that variety of nectars in their diet. To take care of this oasis we had two permanent gardeners. These gardens had become the pride and envy of our mansion. An extra touch was the display between the columns of several hammocks brought directly from Barquisimeto, a Venezuelan area known for its colorful looms, and also some pottery jars that we brought from the Andes. There was also a guest house that was fully equipped.

The mansion was surrounded by a high wall with built-in cameras and guardhouses, since the area was quite dangerous due to the presence and rivalry between drug cartels, the mafia and other criminal activities that Ramiro had promised to put an end to in order to bring peace back to the region. As the first lady, I played a very important representative role, and I would also take on other social responsibilities in support of my husband. That March, I was in charge of entertaining the wives of the governors of the other states. I organized an afternoon of tea and pastries. No, those meetings were not boring at all. On the contrary, we shared very funny anecdotes about our roles as first ladies. Many of us were contemporaries, which helped us to identify better with each other. We tried to hold our meetings once a month, and each time in a different state. That helped me to become more familiar with the geography of this beautiful country.

THE MARKED PREY

ANOTHER TYPE OF MEETING

I remember that one Wednesday Rafael Sanchez came to visit, who was said to be my husband's cousin. Here everyone is called cousins, like in Venezuela everyone is compadres, so I don't really know if they were blood cousins or just social cousins. From his appearance I imagined he was involved in more than shady business. Rafael wore thick, heavy gold chains around his neck, one of them with a heavy crucifix, although I don't think he was very religious, and an authentic Rolex watch that matched the cufflinks on his shirt. Those cufflinks had his initials engraved on them, RS, which he flaunted when he showed them to us with pride as a newly millionaire. I had nicknamed him secretly "Golden Mustache", since he reminded me of those singers from the era of Roberto Cantoral, Los Panchos and Pedro Infante that I had listened to in my early youth.

My sisters, who are a little older than me, were favored with serenades of popular songs brought by their suitors. By the time it was my turn, they had already gone out of fashion or it had become too dangerous to walk the streets after certain hours.

Aside from music, we had little in common with the people of Mexico. Golden Mustache and my husband, Ramiro Ramirez, began meeting in our living room once a week. With aged whiskey in hand, they would drink too many drinks and talk nonsensically. I attributed it to the alcohol loosening their tongues, until I started paying more attention. From the kitchen, I could hear them discussing secret projects that would bring them extraordinary profits they couldn't justify.

When Ramiro was away, his odious cousin would take advantage of the opportunity to flirt with me, and he didn't hide it in the least. That dirty old man was a disgusting, unscrupulous man. That made me extremely angry. I told my husband, but he didn't give it any importance. He told me that was his way of being, and that I shouldn't pay attention to it. They protected each other and watched each other's backs.

One day, they invited Diosdiablo Moreno, an ungraceful and very unpleasant character. He arrived at my house preceded by a group of armed and masked men, who searched our property inside and out, making sure that the place was safe for the meeting. I later found out that Diosdiablo was the leader of Los Caballeros Temporarios, a group of high-caliber criminals that dominated the area. He also represented other gangs, such as El Tren del Arauca, the Salvadores, the Calvos and the Antioqueña family, forming alliances of convenience both locally and internationally. They stayed up telling stories and accounts until dawn. It was preferable that I was not present, so I left without any problem and went to my room to read.

I always had a pending pile on my nightstand, and, depending on my mood, I chose the one that most caught my attention at that moment. I learned not to feel guilty if I left a book unfinished, but I felt like there was so much good reading, and so little time...

I was suspicious of the shady activities that Ramiro's friends were discussing, so I had microphones installed in the living room and kitchen of the house. The recordings reached the veterinary hospital, where I listened to them and carefully transcribed them, to cover my back if necessary. But who could I trust? At least I had my faithful canine companion, Kiana, by my side.

I don't know where Kiana came from, but on my birthday, when I arrived at the veterinary hospital (I was always the first one there), I found a dog transport box on the doorstep. Inside was a Weimaraner puppy. Taped to the box was a card that read, "Thank you, Santa. I know you'll welcome me, and I'll be your best friend. Signed, Kiana."

How could I refuse to adopt her? She looked just like Rhodda, the Weimaraner I had for so many years in Caracas. Was she her reincarnation, if that exists among dogs? Her little blue eyes looked at me, asking me to accept her. I took her out of her cage and picked her up. She wagged her tail as if she were dancing the zamba and, in the process, she peed on me. This time I forgave her.

From that moment on we were inseparable. We arranged a space for her near the door of our room so she could sleep there.

She and Ramiro never got along, but my husband couldn't refuse to let me adopt her, after all, she was my dog, the product of an anonymous gift. In some way, she was already beginning to make up for my loneliness.

FORTITUDE, HEART

I've never been a very good liar; it shows on my face and I can't hide it easily. However, for now, I had no choice. My life would be in danger if I accidentally made an unwelcome comment. I was still the exemplary wife about whom my husband would have no complaints. The machismo that ran through his veins also scared me. I had seen him mistreat the servant women, his secretaries and people who reported that their partners beat them and physically and verbally abused them, something quite common in our environment.

He, as Governor of the State, and in common agreement with his cousin-friend Rafael Sanchez, whom he had appointed as Director of Police, filed away the cases of prominent men in the community in exchange for large bribes. I discovered that Mexico has one of the best laws to protect women from abuse by their partners, but it is also known for its great impunity in cases brought to the police and in the courts.

We lived comfortably and made generous donations to the Church, maintaining cordial relations with it, as it represented one of the most important powers in our devout community. I had to go to mass every Sunday and attend funerals, baptisms and weddings of relatives, friends and acquaintances. It was customary to ask the governor to sponsor a baby here and there, and he already had more than 90 godchildren since he had won the governorship, about whom we knew very little, but who expected special benefits from their "sponsor."

In the city, they began to call me "The Saint," and it was no wonder. All I needed was a halo over my head, but that would be another story. Aside from my duties as a housewife and veterinarian, I decided to create a non-profit organization, oriented toward the social, educational, and cultural well-being of locals and migrants passing through. I consulted with other similar organizations and learned about the financial and legal limitations. I used my husband's contacts as a front for private donations, and no one refused to help (or perhaps it was a form of money laundering for some contributors?).

We organized spectacular galas with orchestras, famous singers, dances, food and drinks to raise funds, and everyone wanted to be invited. There were also silent auctions, raffles and public recognition of donors, except those who preferred to remain anonymous. These parties were recognized as "the social event of the year," where so many friends would meet again. The local press and television stations covered the event. Women wore dresses by well-known designers, and men showed them off like competition trophies. National and international figures were invited to give the gala even more shine.

With the money raised, we built and maintained a shelter for migrants passing through, with the condition that they could only stay for a week at most. During that week, they could at least feel almost at home. The temporary mini-houses were decorated with flags from their countries of origin. Most of them came from Cuba, Venezuela, and Nicaragua. In addition, they were served their typical meals, given clean clothes, shoes, and even some money to continue their journey. They also received medical, dental, psychological, and legal care. As the main representative of the organization, I interviewed them, helped them fill out a questionnaire, and offered them a safe place where they could share, anonymously, their experiences. Some of this data served as statistical support to justify our organization, but the confidential conversations were secret and sacred to me. I did not identify them with names to protect those who told them to me, but I would always remember the faces and expressions of each one of those I had heard. Their words were accompanied by the pain of their experiences.

I learned a lot. Every day in the shelters, my sensitivity and empathy towards those who silenced their cries for justice increased. They were very afraid.

…and then one day…

IF YOU BELIEVE IT, YOU CREATE IT

One day, a whole family arrived at the shelter. I thought it was complete because it included several generations, from grandparents to grandchildren. But where had they come from? And who were they? Their faces and voices were familiar to me.

Suddenly, a light bulb went off, as we say in my country, and I remembered clearly our bond. So much time had passed and the circumstances were so different. The wrinkles, the deformed hands and calloused feet, the dull and dry eyes from crying, surrounded by dark circles on the faces of the new arrivals, made me feel guilty about my privileged position. Their voices, at first silent and fearful, full of horror and pain in their stories, made me relive their experiences in some way, although mine had been somewhat different. My own scars of pain and loss were opening up again.

How could I forget them?

My paradise, where I was born, raised and studied, began to change. At first, the leaders, disguised as good people and elected under promises impossible to keep, stretched out their tentacles to take over the soul of our people. They were long tentacles like those of giant octopuses, with suckers that sucked up everything they could for their own benefit. Expropriations, crimes, disappearances, torture, separation of families and friends were just some of the things they subjected the people to, who had to remain silent. Some of the bodies of the opponents were thrown into rivers infested with caribs, also known as piranhas, which left no trace after finishing their banquets of human flesh.

Not content with what they achieved, they turned my happy people into fearful ones, from generous to careful, from dreamers to those who knew about nightmares that became reality day by day. The dictatorship was like a destructive poison with no antidote, which they applied drop by drop, calculating its effect, before the astonished gaze of the unbelievers who believed that it would never happen in our beautiful country. Many believed in the rulers, and the majority fell into the nets of hunger and misery that mercilessly suffocated them.

I saw things from the outside, from the Mexican land that had adopted me some time ago and where I felt stable and at peace. But I understood that the only constant is change. Now I was facing it again...

When I left Venezuela, I thought it would just be for a vacation in Mexico with my friends. When I found out I would end up moving to Michoacán, I had to find a new home for my dog Pepe, a fabulous Rottweiler with whom I learned to train animals for obedience and defense. At my veterinary clinic in Caracas we offered dog training classes, from puppies to adults, where the owners actively participated. An interactive school. I loved being able to contribute to the well-being of both the animal and its owners.

The family that adopted Pepe became an extension of my own family. Every time I returned to visit Venezuela, I stayed with them, the Rivadeneiras, of Peruvian origin, who had also had to leave their country of origin. The last time I visited them, Pepe already had gray hair and walked with difficulty. We could never forget each other.

That was the family who walked from Caracas, where they could no longer live, or rather, survive. They stayed in the shelter for a few days and then I invited them to move into our house, the Governor's house, in the annex for special guests. I couldn't let them go, at least not yet.

Little by little, they told me in detail about the journey that had not yet ended for some of them. The country they were leaving behind had really been a true paradise, anything would be better than staying in Venezuela. For some, that opportunity had ended prematurely... they had disappeared. With this family, or what was left of it, came others, half-dead and exhausted. Many wondered if so much sacrifice had been worth it. Going back was no longer an option.

THE PIECES OF THE PUZZLE

Our cat Olivia was fascinated by the thousand-piece puzzle I had begun to put together. It was a difficult puzzle, with pieces very similar to each other. The black and white photograph on the box represented an unreachable horizon from the photographer's point of view. For me, it was a way to relax after my days full of surprises and challenges, serving almost as a mental health therapy.

Olivia, like a circus juggler, jumped onto the table and, with one swipe, knocked all the pieces I had managed to fit into place onto the floor. I had already completed the border and had sorted the pieces into shades of grey, dark and light. Unlike what I would have done on other occasions, when I would have gotten angry, this time I laughed a lot. I laughed and laughed, picked up the cat, danced with her and thanked her. I imagine she thought I was a little crazy.

That's life, I told myself, as I picked up each little piece.

I put the puzzle pieces back in the box, to start putting it back together again another time. I looked at the time. Three hours had passed without me noticing, absorbed and mesmerized by the damn puzzle. I guess I needed it. Thanks to the accident with the kitten, I got up, went to the bathroom, washed my face with cold water to clear my mind and proceeded to supervise the preparation of dinner. My husband would be home in an hour.

I went down to the kitchen to make sure everything was ready, and then went to the dining room to check that the table was set with extra dishes for Ramiro's special guests. He had asked me to be discreet. The service staff would go home and I would take care of serving dinner.

The ready-made microphones would connect the conversations to recordings that I would later transcribe in my office. They were strategically placed to record every sound and word from that night's conversations. They were Secret Service-style microphones, tiny and nearly undetectable. I had also installed other microphones in the main office, the library, and even in the bathrooms, where, from behind the door, I could listen in on private and confidential conversations. No one knew I was using them, except the one person I could trust.

I went to take a shower. On the way to the bathroom, I turned my head to see a photo taken at a costume party we went to last year. It was a party to celebrate our identities. People dressed up as pirates, doctors, dinosaurs, whatever they thought was part of their hidden personality. Without thinking much, I dressed up as an angel and my husband, Ramiro, as a devil. How ironic. It was not the time to distract my thoughts.

I dressed up all pretty with my hair down. In my country they would have complimented me, "beautiful little cat," but here, even though we speak the same language, they call me "güerita." Not only do we have our typical words, but also very different customs, cultures, history and food. It was here that for the first time I ate a tortilla similar to our casabe de yuca, and not like the egg tortilla I was used to. They call arepas gorditas, and hallacas tamales. They look alike, but they will never be the same. I feel that the European influence on South American cuisine is stronger there than here in Mexico. One gets used to everything, one adapts. At first I compared, but now I don't anymore. Each one is different, with its good things and not so good things.

I went downstairs. The food was already ready.

The cooks had prepared a delicious chicken mole, which would be served with rice and salad, and for dessert we would have flan with ice cream. The French bread had been ordered early. It was served warm with garlic butter for anyone who wanted it. I looked over everything, I was satisfied.

Almost punctually, Ramiro's guests began to arrive. Before they sat down at the table, they already had glasses of whiskey on the rocks in their hands. Golden mustache was playing with the ice, turning it with his chubby fingers. Diosdevil, vulgar as always, began to tell dirty jokes. The others celebrated and laughed out loud. I didn't find them funny at all.

A third guest, Diosanto Garcia, had arrived from Venezuela on his private plane, without going through customs. He had an international arrest warrant, but they were careful and did not give each other away. They all had skeletons in their closets. Diosanto and Diosdiablo boasted about their names and wondered what their mothers had been thinking when they had given them those names, ha, ha, ha.

Mr. Garcia, also quite unpleasant in his physical appearance, had brought three gift packages for those present, one for each one. Once he was comfortable, he took them out of his right pants pocket and gave them to them. Each package contained a significant sample of pure cocaine that his Cartel de los Astros distributed worldwide with the support of military personnel who also benefited from the business. As a special gesture, each package bore the name of each attendee, accompanied by a tablet and a metal object to distribute the powder and snort it without difficulty. Thus, combining the drug and alcohol, they finally sat down at the table. In addition to these packages, he had also brought a gold bar for each of those present, the result of mining exploitation and environmental destruction in the south of my country. They ate, or rather, swallowed like savages, as if they had been starving. I watched them without saying a word.

The dinner lasted for long, endless hours, at the end of which each attendee apologized as best he could and they all staggered out, almost falling, heading to their respective armored cars, surrounded by bodyguards, with their gold bar hidden under their jackets.

Kiana was growling quietly, discreetly, and she was looking at me with that uncomfortable look. She wanted me to understand that she didn't like the people who had come to the house. I should be careful. Her instincts were rarely wrong. This time, they corroborated mine.

That night Ramiro and I slept in separate rooms.

THE HANGOVER

The day after dinner, after having spent the whole night vomiting, Ramiro woke up in a very bad mood and with an unbearable headache. We had to call his family doctor, who he trusted completely, Dr. Efraín González. Efraín, a handsome, tall, athletic, gray-haired, well-built and very pleasant man, always came home wearing designer ties and his white coat. His leather shoes were always polished. Without thinking much, he examined my husband and diagnosed him with acute withdrawal syndrome: the hangover from a binge combined with some drug. The doctor's recommendations included rest in a dark, quiet room, hydration with chicken broth and a painkiller for the headache. For the public, justifying Ramiro's absence from his office, it was a very strong and contagious virus, a version fully supported by the doctor.

Knowing that he would stay home that day, I left for the veterinary clinic. Another case of severe trypanosomiasis. These cases were no longer so rare, but for me they were starting to become "too many." Three of the recent patients had already arrived as terminal cases. Without asking their owners' permission, I had performed an autopsy on them before cremating them and handing over their ashes. Autopsies were meticulous and I decided to do them myself. I wrote my notes with symbols that no one could recognize. In this way, I began to protect the information about the findings.

In all the cases I examined, I found something very curious. It was a very small device, similar to those I had found in the samples of Benito and Bruno. They were already beginning to look familiar. They resembled the identification microchips that are placed on dogs to help locate their owners in case they get lost. The latest version of these microchips included a GPS to locate them and a recorded sound that called the dog by name, training it to return home when it heard it.

He kept the devices found in autopsies well hidden. He kept them in small glass jars, filled with cotton, which covered them. He put labels on them with a code indicating the date of discovery, so he could follow the clues... Some of these tiny devices seemed to have been deactivated by the gastric juices of the dogs that had ingested them.

And here the second question arose. Where had they come from? Where had they been ingested? Had the dogs been in the same place? How much time had passed? What information did these artifacts carry? Why and for what purpose?

DELEGATING IS THE KEY

The unknowns kept piling up and I couldn't find any answers. I was at a loss, nothing logical occurred to me. Then, one day I woke up very dizzy. Everything was spinning around me and I couldn't walk without leaning on something or someone. A very strange sensation that I couldn't control and that I had never felt before. As they say, there's always a first time for everything.

My housekeeper, Guadalupe, had become my support and my informant of my actions... by direct orders from Ramiro. She was his personal spy. Guadalupe was a woman of indigenous origin, humble, with little education, easily manipulated and almost convinced that if she continued to be the obedient servant and behaved submissively without demanding anything, her place in heaven would be guaranteed. That was how she had interpreted it from the words she heard from the priest of the church, who had also become one of her lovers. It was rumored that the priest José, much loved by his parishioners, was the biological father of some of the babies sold for adoption, since their mothers, mostly indigenous, could not support them. A parallel business that had the seal of the priest's DNA.

Guadalupe, worried about my health, called my husband, who did not hesitate to find Dr. Gonzalez to examine me. They did not take me to the hospital because I am skeptical and stubborn by nature and I refused to go. I was diagnosed with chronic exhaustion, which I understood without complaining. The only treatment: absolute rest, without medications that could speed up my recovery. In other words, resignation. For me, staying in bed, more than a treatment, was a punishment. I felt that every day that passed without me being present to make decisions on almost everything would be a waste of time. However, I had no choice. My body was not responding, I needed a good rest.

I took advantage of the time to think, reorganize, reinvent myself and reevaluate what was happening around me. I remembered my mother's words: "He who takes on too much, squeezes little." She herself was a woman full of energy and projects, willing to face the risks and difficulties in her path. It had to have come from someone, from such a stick, such a splinter, hehe. I couldn't get rid of my maternal genes. Nor did I deviate much from my paternal genes. My father had that gift of good people that made him reach people's hearts with his warm smile, his timely hugs and his philosophical words that avoided unnecessary confrontations.

Guadalupe came into the bedroom with a cup of relaxing herbal tea, a mixture of sage, passionflower, valerian and chamomile. It was a blast for making me sleep. I drank it without any problems and fell asleep for a few hours. I began to feel that my thoughts were falling asleep too, and I didn't like that so much anymore. When Lupe left the room, I went to the bathroom and threw out the contents of the cup. I learned to pretend that I was dizzy and absent-minded, even though I knew that the pain had passed. It helped me listen to conversations of a different kind, between my husband and my maid.

I learned that I would have to trust and delegate some of my projects to others, although I would continue to supervise them closely. This would also give me time to expand my contribution to the community and create educational and work opportunities for those who wanted to take advantage of them.

I began by locating Jesus Aldana, who was in Germany, in charge of the best police dog training school in Berlin. He had trained Pepe (the Rottweiler) and me in Caracas many years ago and had followed his professional career closely ever since. I invited him with all expenses paid and he arrived in a few days. A good investment for everyone. He could not refuse the offer I made him: he would be the director of our exclusive academy. Over time, his experience and good nose for promoting these necessary services would make it the best of its kind on the entire continent. With an emphasis on the different orientations and requirements for the use of canine services, he would have carte blanche to expand the benefits of such a laudable challenge and hire whoever he considered necessary. He would not only train dogs, but also trainers, selected mainly for their empathy towards animals and their ability to work with them. It occurred to us that he could have space to attract young people who had lost themselves in the world of drugs and were in the process of rehabilitation. It would be part of their therapy and a basis for a more promising future. Jesus accepted without hesitation and moved into a house close to the original academy that we had remodeled for his use, with a contract that would not end even if the government passed into other hands. A guarantee that would give him peace of mind regarding his employment status in this ever-changing world. Jesus was incorruptible.

With the help of Beatriz and Luzarelys, with whom I had worked in my land of grace and who possessed extraordinary creative abilities, we created a contact zoo for the community. They would be responsible not only for caring for the animals, but also for educating the population about their care. In addition, they would work together with Jesus and with the inmates of one of the much-needed rehabilitation clinics in our region. We also created another non-profit organization, Funda Kabra, which would educate not only people recovering from drug and alcohol abuse, but also convicts from the Oaxaca penitentiary whose sentences were to be reviewed and reconsidered. They would work in the field of raising goats for meat and milk. Once they were rehabilitated and out of their unfortunate situations, and after having worked with the goats under the supervision of Bea and Luza, they would be helped to obtain agricultural credits through the state government so that they could, initially under supervision, start their small productive farms. This would give them sufficient material and emotional foundation to build a better future and would contribute to the livestock development of the region.

So I began to delegate part of my legacy to people I trusted the most, certain of their ethical, professional, moral and honest values. I extended my hand to them without reservation.

Every Monday I met with Jesús, Beatriz and Luzarelys to hear how everything was going. We analyzed the information we had gathered and made changes as necessary. I also listened to their ideas about the results of the actions and their own undertakings. They were very productive and rewarding meetings. I had managed to leave in the hands of others what I had refused to let go of for so long.

I recognized them as "my warriors." I saw myself reflected in them. I also considered myself a tireless warrior.

However, shelters were more delicate to delegate people to. Although there were people in charge of cleaning, coordinating with medical services, nutrition, psychological help and primary care, I wanted to continue being the one who conducted the exit interviews. I wouldn't delegate that role to anyone. Some secrets I didn't want, and I couldn't share, yet.

AND MY SPECIAL GUESTS

The dizziness disappeared. I felt fine now. I went downstairs to make my own coffee, a routine I never delegated to anyone. I liked to give it my "personal touch." Very dark, black, and then whitened with the foamy fresh milk from the cows on our farm. The aroma, in addition to the caffeine, stimulated me. The smell of good coffee not only reminded me of the Venezuelan coffee offered to anyone who visited your house, a part of our customs, but also of the mornings at my parents' house.

Suddenly I thought of those animated characters who are attracted by certain smells and go towards them almost by magic. I imitated them. They were like calls from God and caresses on the esophagus.

After satisfying my morning craving, I headed to the annex where the new arrivals were staying. They were beginning to feel more relaxed and rested. The little house they occupied was well equipped, with running water, electricity, food, and clean sheets and towels. These basic things had become a luxury in our home country. I convinced them to stay a while longer in the house. It suited Ramiro, because they made me feel like family and I didn't bother him with my opinions and comments. It suited me, too, because I would employ them in some of my projects while I learned more about their odysseys. Everyone won with these arrangements.

At first, we had to deal with bureaucracy to get work permits. My friends had not only had their belongings stolen, but also their identity papers. So we had to start by creating "semi-original" birth certificates, preserving their birth dates but varying their names, so that those who were after them for "treason" would have a harder time finding them. Anyone who decided to leave there to survive was considered a terrorist and a traitor by the regime, including the grandparents who could barely see, hear or walk properly anymore. I wasn't sure they wouldn't be located in the future, but for now.

THE MEETING WITH THE NURSE

As planned, one of the goals of the association that cared for immigrants in transit was to offer them, in addition to housing, food and shelter, the medical care that they all needed. All our migrants would pass through the clinic that offered its exclusive services to our cause. The nurses would fill out the medical records as much as they could, and then a team of doctors would review them and then the patients. They would take the time necessary, without rushing, and with all our unconditional support.

One of the nurses, a big-hearted and very intuitive brunette, had become my friend and confided in me some details that the doctors did not consider important. She asked me to meet her, almost secretly, because she wanted to give me something.

At my request, we met at a public place, Cafeteria La Siciliana, owned by Bruno Lombardi. The cafe had the best cakes and pastries around, and also the best gelatos with an Italian reputation. Giuseppe, the ice cream maker, had graduated from the famous Carpigiani University, which specialized in the elaboration and production of the best ice creams in the world. Mariela, the nurse, and I sat at a small corner table near the main door. I had learned that it was advisable to be near an exit so that we could evacuate the place in case of something unexpected. The tables had red and white checked tablecloths, the cloth napkins were red, and the flowers in the center of the tables were simple arrangements that gave the place a touch of exclusivity. I liked that place very much.

We ordered our snack and chatted as we enjoyed it. Mariela began by asking me not to tell on her. "Why would I do that?" I asked. "Doña Alma," she said, "it's because I feel like I could be in danger if someone found out what I have to tell you."

"Mariela," I said, "if there's one thing life has taught me, it's not to deceive or betray. I've experienced it myself and I wouldn't wish it on anyone."

Mariela was one of the women who had been abused and harassed. Her father and brothers had raped her when she was just a child. At 13, she had tried to commit suicide after an abortion induced with contaminated instruments that left her infertile for the rest of her life. "You can count on me," I told her without reservation.

MARIELA'S SECRETS

Her hands were shaking as she grabbed her cup of coffee. She accidentally spilled it on the table. Another cup was brought to her. I told her again not to worry, to calm down and act as naturally as possible so as not to arouse suspicion. "Breathe, calm down."

"It's just that what I'm going to tell you is very difficult," she told me.

I asked her to address me informally. It would make communication easier. "I'm listening."

She then handed me a cotton ball inside one of those little boxes that jewelers use. She asked me not to open it there, in public. She began to tell me about its contents.

"That little box, Doña Santa, has a ... I don't know how to describe it. It's like a little piece of metal that I've found on many of the patients we see in the clinic. Coincidentally, the ones who have them all come from Venezuela. Not knowing what they were, and since they looked like foreign bodies almost under the skin, I would take them out before the doctors arrived. Justifying the small wound I had caused, I would say that they had ticks. Some, by the way, did have real ticks that caused them a lot of discomfort, and when I removed them, I would keep them in jars to show the doctors."

"Furthermore, when I asked them about their medical records, they told me that at the border with Colombia they had to go through a 'health check' at one of the National Guard posts. There they were given 'vaccinations', which were understood to be the usual ones. Not all of them were, but they were all vaccinated. The other immigrants from neighboring countries did not have these devices."

I didn't know what to answer, I didn't have an answer at that moment.

He also mentioned to me that the migrants who arrived in the worst physical condition also had a scar near their waist, some on the right side and others on the left. What was the common story? It turns out that almost all of those who came walking from Venezuela, passing through Colombia, Panama and other Central American countries were assaulted, beaten, raped, robbed. They arrived with nothing. They had lost everything, including the will to live. 'The coyotes', people who were supposed to be their guides and protectors, were in cahoots with all kinds of mafias. They were experts in extortion. Since they knew that their clients were already at their wits' end, they offered them the opportunity to sell one of their kidneys, for which they would be paid well and would take care of them until they recovered. These same coyotes would charge them that same money in order to continue protecting them for the rest of the trip. When people were at the end of their desire to continue, they accepted the offer. They took them to the basement of the clinic where my doctor, Dr. Gonzalez, a great friend of my husband, worked, who, in the future and after many investigations, would turn out to be one of the professionals most involved in organ trafficking. That was the other side of Efrain, from a compassionate doctor to an unscrupulous and villainous doctor. When they went overboard with the anesthesia, they took advantage of the opportunity to remove from the bodies not only the two kidneys, but also the liver and other transplantable organs. The human corpses would later be food for domestic animals. Those who survived were thrown out into the street, near our center, at the mercy of God. The strongest survived.

We finished our snack. Something occurred to me that might start to clear up the situation. It was still early. I asked Mariela to accompany me home. I introduced her to my friends and asked her to check them out, since they hadn't yet gone through what the others at the shelter had.

She examined them in detail and surprise! They all had that "special tick" that was not a tick. They all agreed that they had been given the necessary vaccines for traveling, by order of the Guard and the supervision of an agent who said he worked for "El Niño." Between the two of us, and with an animal surgery kit that I always had with me, we removed the artifacts. I put them away along with the little box that Mariela had given me. My friends then went to rest. I thanked Mariela and took her back to her house, on the outskirts of the city.

Until that moment I had not realized the tangle I was getting myself into. The ticks were still active.

WHEN I CAME HOME

Ramiro was waiting for me to have dinner together. I hadn't been expecting him because he was supposed to go to dinner with his cousin, but that meeting was cancelled without my knowledge. He didn't let me know. When I arrived, I wasn't welcomed. My husband was a controlling sexist and preferred to know everything about me: where was I? With whom? Why? He wanted me to tell him everything in great detail.

For me, this behavior was unacceptable and I interpreted it as a lack of trust. Instead of answering his questions, I began to tell him, very calmly at first, that I did not accept his attitude. The responses from both sides escalated in temperature and caliber, and when his anger reached the limit of being uncontrollable, he raised his right hand in the form of a fist and hit me, leaving me with a black eye and my left arm fractured when I tried to protect my face after the first blow. We no longer listened to each other, we insulted each other with all the words we knew. I was surprised not only by his violence, but also by my uncontrolled rage. I had never been physically abused by anyone, and this was unacceptable.

His driver and one of his bodyguards took me to the Jardines de Paz Clinic, a well-known private clinic that was careful not to report this incident to the police. It would be an unacceptable scandal. In any case, the case would have been shelved like so many others.

I did not appear in public for a few weeks until the marks on my face disappeared or could be covered with a good make-up. The explanation for the broken arm was that I had slipped in the entrance of the house…

It wasn't just my arm that was broken. It was also the silent and irreparable fracture of the little that was left in my heart, of the little respect I still had for him, and of the memory of what he had once been, and was no longer. The screams of that night still reverberate in my head like echoes that I cannot silence.

From then on, I tried to avoid my husband, even though his guilt drove him to shower me with gifts, flowers, and jewelry to get me to forgive him. He swore that he would never do it again. For me, once had been more than enough, and I made it very clear to him, but we had signed a contract to represent the governor until the end of the term and I would honor it. I had to look my best. The representation expenses were covered without any limitation. I also made it clear to him that we would no longer have any communication as a couple, and that as soon as his term as governor ended, each of us would go our own way.

Guadalupe, the same maid/housekeeper who had taken care of me previously, took care of me again while I recovered from this new blow. This time I noticed she looked a little haggard. The dark circles under her eyes said more than the words coming out of her mouth. Little by little I managed to get her to talk to me. Lupita had been trying to hide her new condition for several months. Crying, she told me that she was pregnant, that she was very afraid that we would fire her from work, and by the way...

Who was the father of the child? Even she didn't know. There was more than one possibility.

I HAD TO FIND

After our fight, Ramiro assigned me a bodyguard he trusted the most to take care of me and keep me company at all times. José Rafael submitted a daily report to my husband that included details such as where I went, who I met, at what time, and even a copy of the bills for what I bought, including underwear, hair salon, and weekly spa visits. I didn't know that, but I suspected it. So I got him to trust me enough to tell me things about Ramiro, promising him that they would never come out of my mouth.

I found out about the reports he was submitting to his boss by pure chance. It was one day, after several months of taking care of me, when I told him a little white lie that he believed and told my husband. Hehehe, I had caught him, as they say, red-handed. This premeditated gossip would have interesting consequences. The gossip implied that I was planning a surprise trip to Cancun. When I got home, Ramiro asked me about the trip to Cancun. At that moment I realized that José Rafael not only told Ramiro everything, but he also put him in a difficult position when I told him that I was testing the bodyguard's loyalty to him. In reality, I had no trip planned.

Shortly after, I gave Guadalupe prenatal leave, since the little belly she was trying to hide was already showing. She didn't want anyone to know about the baby. Two months later, I told Ramiro that Lupita had had a baby who looked very similar to him, although they say that all babies look alike, and she had even registered him in her town with the name José R. José after the priest and R., I think after my husband, since she wasn't sure who the father was and, in her ignorance, she wanted to please all the possible fathers. Did I say José? Wouldn't the bodyguard, José Rafael, also be a third candidate? It was a real mess. She didn't believe me and swore that she had never deceived me and, by the way, she thought that I had believed her.

THE CASE OF THE BABY AS A DISTRACTION

In the end Ramiro had to confess to me that he had his encounters with Lupita. He had no choice. I didn't really care, but I could use it as blackmail in the future. Lupe would return to our house with her baby when she recovered, and we would find out who the biological donor of half of her genes was. In the meantime, she would be protected at all times and made to believe that her child was welcome in our home. After all, there was a high probability that she could have my husband's blood.

That week there was a meeting of the wives of all the governors of the states of Mexico. These meetings connected me socially with other women who had responsibilities similar to mine, and I had become good friends with Cristina, the wife of the governor of the state of Yucatan. We had visited each other on a few occasions. At snack time I asked her if, by any chance, she was looking for a domestic helper and explained Lupita's situation. My idea was to relocate Guadalupe and her baby away from Michoacan, where she would not be pressured by any of the possible parents of her baby. She had good references, was hard-working and humble.

Cristina hired her and I drove her to Mérida, the capital of Yucatán. Our cities were 1,600 kilometers apart. Without Lupe noticing, I took some saliva samples from the baby, which I would later send to the Genetics Department for analysis. I also took saliva samples from the priest, who had come to visit the house, from the other José, and from my husband, identified with made-up names to keep the secret. Whose DNA would it match?

All of this helped me to tell Ramiro that I neither wanted nor needed bodyguards. Since then, I knew that they were still watching me, but from a distance. Then, by chance, I met Orlando Cisneros at a cybersecurity and artificial intelligence conference in our capital. Orlando, who also worked undercover for the DEA, presented himself as an expert in Mexican National Security. From the first moment, I had a good feeling, but I would have to make sure first that we could collaborate without reservations. Time proved me right.

The day came when I met Orlando and showed him the little box with the famous "ticks" that I had destroyed with a hammer, as I suspected that they were search and encounter devices. A second little box held the gadgets I had found in the autopsies of the deceased dogs. Putting them together, I realized that they were quite similar, almost identical. I had my own ideas about what these artifacts could represent, but they were only premature speculations. Orlando listened to me, perplexed, perhaps as much as I was as I related each case to him. We needed to consider as many options as possible. We also needed to keep our encounters as discreet as possible.

I suggested that we expand our team with Miguel Gonzalez, the owner of Benito, that first German Shepherd with whom I began my new journey. Orlando, however, asked me to be patient. He wanted to investigate Miguel's criminal record first before including him in our group. We could no longer afford to make mistakes that could cost us our lives.

THEY KEPT COMING

Migrants continued to arrive in greater numbers. Our shelter had a limited number of spaces and we had to reduce the number of days they could stay. This also forced us to do our work more expeditiously. We hired two more nurses, as well as cleaning and kitchen staff, two dentists, a doctor and a psychologist, the latter a woman. Some migrants refused to speak to a man. I would continue to do the exit interviews.

THE CALL OF ORLANDO

The phone rang while I was interviewing my last refugee of the day. I didn't answer the call. It rang again and I silenced the phone.

These interviews were heartbreaking. I wanted to do much more to alleviate the pain they expressed, which was also my pain. The suffering that one carries under one's skin is indescribable.

I didn't like to interrupt interviews. This one in particular was a conversation full of details. My interviewee showed no emotion on his face. He looked as if he had been robbed of more than the money and documents he was carrying. If you could see his heart, it would be as if a bulldozer had been used to empty it, like a pumpkin when you've removed its inner contents. The man had a vacant look on his face, he had seen too much. He had lost everything, his horizon, his hope, his desire.

I took a breath and asked him to do the same. We both calmed down and drank some water filtered from a jar I had brought from my homeland. Ramón looked at it and remembered that they had a very similar one at home. He told me that he felt like he was drinking holy water. I thought the same thing too, since the water here was undrinkable.

One day, despite being warned not to drink unfiltered water, I thought it was an exaggeration. I remember it was one of those super hot days and Ramiro, Kiana and I went for a walk. The city had public drinking fountains and I took the risk of drinking water from one of them. Within two hours I was in the hospital, shivering, with acute gastroenteritis and extreme dehydration, and with a bottle of Lactated Ringer's connected to an IV in my left arm. I was kept there for observation for two days. It was a very unpleasant experience, but I learned to be careful not to drink public water.

Ramón and I resumed the interview.

Among other things, Ramón told me that he had left with his wife Josefina, who was pregnant, and their three-year-old daughter from Trujillo, a beautiful Andean state. It was hard for them to make the decision to leave Venezuela, but the situation had become unsustainable. They packed what they considered essential in their backpacks, and with that they left for the United States, where his sister-in-law, Josefina's sister, lives. There they could start over, little by little, building a better future for the family.

Ramon, however, had arrived alone. Where were his wife and daughter? When I asked him, he collapsed in tears. He cried and cried. I had never seen anyone cry for so long, without stopping, until his eyes, exhausted, closed for a while. I told him there was no hurry. On the contrary, I asked him to stay here a few more days, while he recovered. I could not and should not, humanly, let him leave in that state. I asked him to go and rest, and that we would talk the next day, in the afternoon.

Then I remembered that I had received some calls and had not answered them. I checked the phone, but I did not find any known or repeated numbers. Who had it been? Why so much mystery? I had no way of tracing the calls.

The next day, at about 8 a.m., when I was already at the veterinary clinic, the phone rang again. I didn't know who it was, there was no identification. I decided to answer it. Orlando told me that he had called me the day before. I apologized. I don't normally answer calls whose origins I can't identify, other than that I was busy with Ramon's interview. He told me that he would change his number frequently because he didn't want to be discovered. He told me that he preferred that we meet in person. My phone could be tapped.

So we decided to change strategy.

"I have news for you," he said.

"Good or bad?"

"It depends," he replied.

"With regard to Miguel, carte blanche. He is an honest man, committed to justice, incorruptible. We can count on him."

When he told me that, I felt a chill. My trusted team was beginning to solidify, but we had to be VERY discreet. That was the good news.

"And the bad ones?"

"The bad ones are very bad." He was referring to the famous "ticks" that were embedded in the bodies of walkers, and that we had also found in the autopsies of dogs that had died of trypanosomiasis.

"Soul," he said. "The matter is extremely complicated and very interesting. It turns out that it is a very sophisticated device. It had been designed using Advanced Artificial Intelligence. The military forces of a group of international allies had joined together to produce them for the purpose of spying on enemies. They sent signals to satellites orbiting the earth. Thus, they were already using them to locate enemies and annihilate them in special missions. And speaking of enemy spies, that group had detected some flaws in their controls. Apparently a person with a high military rank, who was not suspected of being related to any other type of activities, had been sharing confidential information with unscrupulous people. These people, who spared no expense and had plenty to cover them, hired corrupt scientists, whom they paid millions of millions to be able to copy and reproduce the devices. They also already had a few satellites of their own orbiting the earth."

Alma wasn't quite understanding all that technological information, but that's what her new team was there for.

"Orlando," I asked, "and how does everything you're telling me relate to the situation of migrants?"

"I'm still trying to put things together," he told me. "When I have everything clearer, we'll meet again. Meanwhile, on your part, keep gathering information with your interviews. Now, write them down in symbols that only we can understand."

And so Alma continued and also created an interactive language using a combination of the Morse Code she had learned when she was a child and part of the Scout group, with some symbols created especially by her. Orlando, Miguel and she would use this method of communication between them.

THE MARKED PREY

ALL SAINTS DAY

Here in Michoacán it is celebrated every year on the first of November. That day coincides with the arrival of the monarch butterflies that come migrating from the north at this time of year. The locals think that they are the spirits of their loved ones who come to visit. It is a popular celebration with a lot of meaning. Flowers, music, food, parades, catrinas, candles, We took advantage of that day to meet the three of us at the Municipal Cemetery, all in our traditional costumes and masks so that we would not be recognized. We sat next to a tombstone identified with the number 512. I remember that number in particular because I had dreamed about it repeatedly, but I didn't know if it meant anything. I let it go. Until that moment I couldn't find any connection. It turned out that it would be one of the places for our meetings, just that.

Miguel, Orlando and I began to draw up our first map of ideas that we would expand upon as we accumulated more information. We wanted to find the heart of this whole mess. Who was behind all this mystery, and why? To have control, power and money, using migrants as their playing pieces, or as their trading cards. I'll give you this card in exchange for this other one, do you have it? As Machiavelli said in his youth, back in the year 1500, " the end justifies the means ." A few years have passed since then and it seems as if we haven't evolved one micron, I thought to myself.

For me, migration began to take on the nuances of modern slavery. The new slaves are free, but they are anchored by pain and need. They are humiliated and mistreated, they are used and discarded.

For now, Miguel would be in charge of finding the place where the dogs that arrived sick had been. He would also look for coincidences, if there were any, with the food that was being provided to the animals.

Orlando would be in charge of investigating more about the devices that were manufactured in Nuevo León and everything related to them, the original partners of the business and those who had joined over time. Inventories, origins and destinations of the merchandise would be part of his work.

And I would continue with my interviews and analyze the information received, especially regarding the similarities and differences between the number of people who began their career until the moment they arrived here.

We would meet again in two weeks. There was no time to lose. Things were getting more and more complicated.

MARIELA

My trusted nurse began to feel that she was being watched at the health center. In order not to arouse suspicion, she let some patients with the famous ticks embedded in them through, while keeping a secret diary identifying them. The pre-selection, for now, consisted of extracting the artifacts from young people under 40 years old. She would deliver them to me at the Sanctuary of the Virgin of Guadalupe. Mariela, who is very devoted to the Virgin, was also my ally. José, the priest who met with my husband, was the parish priest of that church. Hidden, he watched us from a confessional that was not in use, but Kiana, who always accompanied me, approached and began to wag her tail, recognizing the priest's scent. The dog was more agitated than usual. José came out of his "hiding place," pretending that he had just finished the day's confessions, with a little notebook in his hand. We had not seen a single parishioner confess.

Before saying goodbye to Mariela, who was sitting in one of the last pews in the church, near the exit gate, I told her: "Friend, don't expose yourself anymore. It's not necessary and I don't want you to arouse suspicions. I don't need any more ticks." I thanked her with a big hug and the promise that I would protect her.

Once a week, Father José celebrated a special mass for the migrants and blessed them from the pulpit. During one of these masses, I went into the sacristy, found the notebook, and photographed it. I left it as it was and left without anyone noticing my presence. I immediately sent the photos to Orlando and deleted them from my cell phone. I did not want to leave any trace of my inexperience in these strange matters.

TWO WEEKS LATER

The two weeks we had planned passed very quickly. Orlando, Miguel and I met again at the cemetery. I gave Orlando the metal ticks that Mariela had collected. After explaining the case to him, I asked him to send one of his agents to protect her. He agreed without hesitation.

His concern increased when he examined the artifacts I had given him. He discovered that some were still active. A critical and serious error! It was a failure that we could not have avoided, since we were completely unaware of their scope.

In addition to the gadgets, I gave Miguel a copy of the priest's black notebook. Orlando had already received it. I also handed over the report with all the information I had gathered during my interviews.

Miguel told us that he had found some very interesting and significant information. He would explain it to us later. We couldn't stay there a minute longer.

The tension in the air was palpable. The feeling of being followed intensified with each step. From that moment on, everything changed.

RAMIRO

My husband asked me to be more present in official affairs. I should be more visible, showing myself as the selfless wife involved in social programs that helped the most needy. It was in his interest to have a good image, since new elections for public offices were approaching and his intention was to win the governorship again. Although this was not provided for in the State laws, they managed to modify them. The group of legal advisors of the current administration changed them without consultation, allowing reelection and granting life titles. In any case, the elections were also rigged and there was no way to verify the real results. Everything was being systematically manipulated. The small group of leaders and their accomplices had all the power.

My duties included appearing at public meetings. At one of them, one of my husband's closest collaborators was addressing the audience. Ramiro was at his side and I was at his side. Suddenly, I fell to the floor. I lost consciousness, and when I woke up, I was in the hospital where I had already undergone surgery. A bullet had hit my left shoulder, just millimeters from the jugular vein. I was alive by a miracle. Speculations swirled around my husband's political enemies and opponents: that it had been a sniper, that it had been someone in the audience. Television and radio stations came to interview me at the hospital. The media manipulated the information in such a way that the people of Michoacán thought that a miracle had occurred because I was still alive. Most of them went to vote on election day thinking that God had wanted them to save me, and Ramiro took over the governorship again. They organized the inauguration, or rather a retaking of the inauguration as if it were the coronation of some king whom everyone had to obey. They spared no expense and had plenty of money to cover it. Drugs, alcohol, food and music were all over the city. It looked like a patronal festival. I only attended the official ceremony, but I did not take part in the festivities. Although I had already recovered from the attack, I did not want to take unnecessary risks.

PRIVATE INVESTIGATIONS

Orlando and Miguel continued to investigate the pending issues. They added another one to the list: the attempted murder of Ramiro, his collaborator, or mine. I wasn't quite sure. Even stranger things were happening.

The bodies of Mariela and the bodyguard who looked after her appeared in the underground rivers of Cacahuamilpa, closed to the public at this time of year. They were discovered by one of the cadaver dogs who graduated from our academy. We started looking for her when she did not show up for work for a few days, which surprised us a lot because she was very responsible and conscientious. Nothing was known about her bodyguard either. Her autopsy revealed that she had been tortured and raped by several individuals before the coup de grace that ended her life. It also revealed that some of her organs were missing: both kidneys, the liver and the lungs. The body of Raúl, the bodyguard, was also missing some organs. This indicated that within the group that had participated in these terrible crimes there was, at least, someone who knew what to do with the organs. Semen samples were also taken from Mariela's vagina. Semen from four different individuals was sent to specialized DNA laboratories, and, of course, also controlled by the Police Department. We had some trusted people everywhere, and we secretly obtained copies of the results. We knew who they had been, and who their bosses were, all very close to my family.

The heads of both bodies were found in another location, not far from where the bodies had been found. The heads were inside black plastic bags, with notes attached to them that read: "Next will be yours. Take care, we are watching you." Although the notes did not have a specific name written on them, I took them as if they had been addressed to me.

I was in deep pain. I had grown very fond of Mariela. At first I was paralyzed by the news. I refused to accept what had happened. Mariela had been one of the pillars that supported me, and she had collapsed. In some ways I compared it to the death of my mother, the most important pillar in my family. When I finally internalized what had happened, I recognized the feeling of definitive physical loss and the frustration of not having done more. I felt somehow guilty about their deaths.

The bodies of Raúl and Mariela were cremated after the autopsies. The perpetrators did not want to leave any more clues that could implicate them. They changed the autopsy report, although we had already obtained copies of the originals. The pathologist disappeared from the scene. He was never heard from again.

GUADALUPE RETURNED

It had been a long time since Guadalupe had gone to work with my friend Cristina, the wife of the governor of Yucatan. Since the gubernatorial elections had recently taken place, and in Merida they had changed their governor, Lupita's services were no longer needed. She also wanted to return to Michoacan. I welcomed her and her little son back to the mansion.

Ramiro seemed pleased with her arrival. She had changed somewhat. Her body was fuller and so was her head. While she was there, my friend Cristina also helped her finish her studies at school. She also took a traditional cooking course in which she learned how to buy and choose the best ingredients, to prepare and serve them with grace and elegance, which we put to good use here at the special dinners we hosted at home. I loved her creativity in cooking and, when I had a little time left, I would go into the kitchen to learn from her. That also helped me calm down a bit.

Typical Mexican food was quite different from ours, especially it is much spicier, as they say here. Also the names of some fruits and vegetables are different.

THE MARKED PREY

Lupita's return also brought back some memories, things I hadn't thought about in a while. She had locked away her little boy's DNA results after receiving and reading them. A card up her sleeve that she would use when it was convenient.

On the other hand, the Rivadeneiras, the family that I had hosted in the house next to ours, were able to become independent and moved to the outskirts of Morelia, to a small farm that produced avocados. They continued to work for me, but without my constant supervision. I liked that.

Little by little, the pieces of the imaginary puzzle fell into their holy place.

A NEW CALL

It rang only once. Once was the time to find out who it was. Time, day and place waiting. My anxiety and nervousness levels increased when they left me in limbo. I tried to keep myself busy so it wouldn't be noticeable. I went to the weekly mass for the pilgrims. There, while they were passing the basket of offerings, a piece of paper stuck out from underneath and the person who was guiding it told me, very discreetly, to grab it. I squeezed it in my hand and left the church. I crossed the street and entered my favorite cafe, Giuseppe's and his ice cream. While they prepared me a hot chocolate, thick, just the way I like it, and a croissant, I went to the bathroom. There I felt safe. I opened my hand to unfold the paper I had received at the church. I read it, memorized it and threw it in the water. I flushed the toilet so as not to leave a trace of its contents. I washed my hands and returned to my table, where the cup of chocolate I had ordered was already waiting for me. I dipped the croissant into the hot chocolate, even though my parents had told me that you didn't do that in public. I ate it with gusto and drank the chocolate with the greatest of pleasure. I remembered my last meeting with Mariela, here. How I miss her!

The meeting was to take place in half an hour, right there in the cafeteria. I would meet Silvia, who would pretend to be a friend from long ago. I didn't know her, but we both pretended that we were like "thieves and grime" as always. Silvia had been sent by Orlando. Thin and tall, like the model in the magazines he worked for to distract attention, he was also a very well disguised undercover agent. We had a short and precise conversation.

We stood up, hugged each other like the friends we pretended to be, and left. Each of us went her own way.

IT WAS STILL DAYLIGHT

I went to the Rivadeneiras' little house. There I met Orlando. We went outside to the patio, where no one could hear us. He had very important information and I also had many things to tell him.

First, he noticed a small bump near the scar I had after the bullet was removed. It looked a lot like the famous ticks. Of course, they had been put there during surgery. Since I could feel the scar, and I couldn't see it in the mirror, I thought it was just part of it.

We decided to talk in silence, in code, using paper and pencil that we would destroy at the end of the meeting. We also decided to keep the tick on my neck, knowing what it was. That way we would have the enemy at hand.

Orlando started with the report about the DNA found in Mariela's autopsy. "Are you ready to hear it?" he asked me. I nodded. I knew it wouldn't be good news. I took a deep breath.

He had obtained the original autopsy reports, which were later altered. The missing medical examiner was never found. The DNA belonged to three nurses and one of the doctors at the clinic where the migrants were examined. The doctor's DNA belonged to Dr. Efraín González. They were all part of the team that Mariela had belonged to. The matter did not end there. Orlando had all four followed. They happened to work in the basement of the hospital where I had been taken after the attack. There was an organ bank there that would be sold for transplants, a business that had become very lucrative due to high demand and low supply. One more contraband operation. Donors were scarce, but not for this group.

He had also discovered something else.

I had had enough with what he had told me for now. Orlando told me no, I had to listen to the rest of the information he had for me. It was about ticks.

I couldn't imagine what he would say to me next.

I was ready to listen.

It turns out that the micro-sensors were produced in Nuevo Leon, in the same factory where other military devices were made. A special division had been created there that had the most modern and specialized technology that existed at that time. Diosdiablo Moreno and Rafael Sanchez, my husband's cousin, were partners in this company. Two types of micro devices were produced there, all connected to the satellites that were already in orbit. The first type had the initials RS, those of the famous cousin. In this case, they were not only the initials of Rafael's last name, but also those of my husband: Ramirez Sanchez. The second ones had the number 512, the same number that had appeared in my dreams.

Almost all of the 512 production was sent to the border between Venezuela and Colombia, where the El Tren del Arauca gang operated. It was at this border crossing where vaccines and "the other vaccines" were administered, that is, the 512. This tiny object included information about the migrant as well as a GPS so that they could be located wherever they were. All of this information was analyzed in another computer center that would classify each migrant according to future needs. Some of this group would also be given a second device, the RS, whose carriers would be forced to be "mules," trafficking drugs that they would be made to swallow in a kind of small condom, almost impossible to detect and that they would pick up, eventually, after crossing the border with the United States. They were not only carrying cocaine, but also fentanyl, the fashionable drug that was killing so many people in the north.

The tick-stained devices were also applied to migrants from other countries. In short, migration had become the "business of the century." For every migrant leaving Venezuela, the dictator, his partner Diosanto, and some high-ranking military officers collected a juicy sum of money. The more chaotic the situation in the country, the more people would leave in search of a better future. Thus, the violence of the forces of law and order against the population increased. Many of the prisoners who were relatively unknown had been sent to the border. Also, other more privileged ones trained for special missions had been mixed in among the Venezuelan migrants, with valid passports created on an island north of Venezuela. Many of these migrants were of Iranian origin and from other terrorist groups. They would be untouchable and would be protected by certain mafias throughout their journey to the north, where they would enter without difficulty.

It was getting dark and I had to get home before Ramiro arrived. He didn't like me not being home for dinner.

Before we said goodbye, I asked Orlando to take the Rivadeneiras to a safe place. My tick would probably have already indicated to my followers where I was. The farm was immediately abandoned and my friends, whom I never saw again, were taken to another place. I never asked about them again, but I would always carry them in my heart.

ASSIMILATING

Kiana, the dog, my faithful companion, seemed more confused than ever and did not move from my side. She was protecting me. She sensed something, and as always, she was right. Many changes were happening and my personal floor seemed to be quicksand. My peace was on red alert.

Miguel, who reported directly to Orlando, had also discovered things that did not fit into our limited capacity for reasoning. It turned out that, since there was a shortage of concentrated dog food, the owners of some of the dogs formed a cooperative to solve the nutritional problems, and created a special butcher shop for animals. In this cooperative butcher shop, viscera, bones and other products of dubious origin were sold, some of animal origin, beef, pork, chicken... and others of... The other meats, human skins and other viscera came from the hospital where the organ bank was located. Some of the meats still contained traces of "the ticks" that the nurses had forgotten to destroy. And the viscera, some, were infected with the trypanosome mutant. It sounded quite unreal and macabre...

How had they gotten there?

THE FIRST SELECTION

From the interview with Ramón I obtained the following story.

Ramón, his wife Josefina and their little daughter had been walking for several weeks and were at the crossing between Colombia and Panama. They were going slowly. Fina was pregnant with her second baby and her legs hurt, they were quite swollen and her shoes were tight.

The Darien Gap area that all migrants had to cross was also known as the green hell. Extremely dangerous, humid and hot, jungle-like, full of mosquitoes, snakes, spiders and scorpions , jaguars and pumas and congas, a giant poisonous ant whose sting produced neurological disorders for which there was no antidote. People stung by these ants died in convulsions and in great pain. As if that were not enough, mafias of drug traffickers, guides and human traffickers and many other things shared the loot of the migrants who had to pass through that place. The pilgrims were nothing more than exchangeable, negotiable tokens. Young women and girls were separated and suffered sexual violence from the group on duty. Not only were they raped, but they were also separated, microchipped with 512 and sent to places where they would serve as sexual slaves. One of those victims was Josefina, who was attacked in front of her husband Ramón and her little daughter. The violent abuse by the seven men who raped her ruptured her uterus. She and the baby she was carrying bled to death. They also mistreated her little daughter and then took her away crying and screaming, who knows where. No wonder Ramón had no tears left.

Another group of young people, selected for their good physical condition, were also separated from the group and offered to work as "mules" in exchange for protection from the families they had left behind. If they did not accept, they would kill their loved ones who had been left behind. Almost all of them had to say yes, swallow the plastics full of drugs and run the risk of dying if a capsule broke inside their body. Upon arriving in Michoacán they were taken to the basement of the hospital where they would have their stomachs pumped and where the drugs would be received. Unfortunately, their story did not end there. Exhausted as they were, most of them no longer had the will to live. They were transported to another department where they were calmed down, anesthetized and their organs were removed to be the inventory of the organ bank for transplants. The remains of the bodies were thrown into garbage containers and then taken to the cooperative butcher shop.

Ramón had been a little luckier. He escaped after seeing what had been done to his wife and daughter, hid for a few days, and slowly moved through the jungle without being detected, or caught. He was detected, yes, but they were not interested in him at all. He was thin, malnourished, and showing signs of early dementia. He was like a walking piece of garbage.

When he finally made it to Mexico and to our shelter, we let him rest and recover for several days. He didn't want to stay here for long. His testimony helped to clarify many questions. The pieces of the puzzle kept finding their place.

I made an appointment with Silvia, the model. We met again at my favorite coffee shop. There I asked her to escort and protect Ramón until he could cross the northern border. Express asylum would be granted to him for obvious humanitarian reasons and for having helped with such important information. They complied and he was able to reunite with his sister-in-law.

A REVELATION

The night before Children's Day, Ramiro and I were at home. Guadalupe had prepared a dinner for us that would leave you wanting to lick your fingers. While we were eating, I don't even remember what we were talking about, when suddenly my husband, filled with uncontrolled rage, began to insult me in the rudest way I had ever heard. He got up from the table and complained about my adventures that he had been monitoring in detail. He asked me about Orlando and Miguel, who they were, if they were my lovers, if they were assholes, a capital insult in Mexico, if they were this or that. He was about to hit me when Kiana jumped on him and bit his hand. I think that with that bite a finger came off, the middle finger of his right hand, which I had to take out of the dog's mouth. I sent the finger with my husband and the driver, who immediately went to the hospital emergency room. There they glued it back on. I understand that he would need a lot of physical therapy to regain movement in his bruised finger. I did not accompany him. I locked myself in my bedroom and did not come out until the next day, for the parties.

Before leaving, I had taken the envelope containing the DNA results of Lupita's son out of the safe. I intended to show them to Ramiro when we returned from the festival.

PREPARING FOR CHRISTMAS

The government had an annual Christmas program. They called it the Children's Day Celebration. All kinds of gifts, clothing and candy were collected for the children of the region throughout the year. The largest park in the city was the setting for these celebrations and all the children of the city were invited, regardless of their ethnic, social, economic or educational status. We had made a census that we updated annually with the help of maternity wards and local schools, and we knew the names, ages, tastes and needs of each boy and girl. The gifts would even have individual cards with the names of each of the children. The entire area was covered with kiosks with music and food, contests and games. A circus was also hired and there were contests of all kinds. At the end of the afternoon a large Christmas tree was lit and Christmas carols were sung. It was a very special day and expected by the population. There would be no alcohol of any kind. It was a healthy party.

In short, it was the great celebration of pride of the government.

I liked it a lot because it reminded me of the celebration of Children's Day throughout

Venezuela, where I had been a volunteer for many years.

Once the lights were turned on, the Christmas tree, a beautiful pine tree brought from Alaska, the mariachis began to sing songs that we all knew and we accompanied them with our voices. I was in the middle of that when…

I never heard from him again. They covered my head with a black bag and took me out of the party. They threatened me and told me to stay calm, not to shout. I heard them say, "Get to the gabacho, get to the gabacho! Quick, he has to be there before dawn."

Kiana was with me the whole time because I kept her on a leash. Despite all the bad things, she was one of the few good things.

FINALLY, THE HOOD IS REMOVED

I don't know what day it was, what time it was, or how much time had passed since I was kidnapped. They must have injected me with some kind of tranquilizer because I don't remember anything. Kiana was still by my side. They had taken good care of her.

I began to open my eyes little by little. Where was I? Who was I with?

PART TWO

MY GOD, WHERE AM I?

At least Kiana, my faithful Weimaraner, was by my side. She started licking my left hand that was hanging on the side of the bed. I think that was what finally started to wake me up. When I finally woke up, I was very disoriented. I had no idea what had happened or where I was at that moment. Everything was unknown. I didn't know what day it was or what time of day it was, and even less, what I was doing there. The last thing I remember was being at the Children's Fair in Michoacán. The music of the mariachis was still ringing in my ears, the smell of fried food was stuck to the clothes I was wearing, blue jeans, a white shirt and my medal with the Virgin of Guadalupe on one side, and the Virgin of Coromoto on the other side, the patron saints of Mexico and Venezuela.

A few minutes later there was a knock at the door. Kiana started barking, warning me and still protecting me. With my hoarse voice, still half asleep, and like a whisper, I answered.

"Well?"

"May I come in?" said a familiar voice.

"One moment, please."

At least I wanted to brush my hair. My leather briefcase was on the table in the small dining room of the suite where I was. I opened it. I had everything in there, and of course my toothbrush. I went to the bathroom and tidied myself up as best I could.

I opened the curtains and noticed that it was daytime. I didn't recognize any of the buildings I could see from the window. I also noticed that Kiana had food and water.

I finally approached the door. I opened it cautiously. Kiana, attentive, began to move her tail and her hips as if she were dancing a rumba. She was delighted and so was I. The dog recognized Orlando, whom she loved very much.

Musiú, the nickname by which he was known among his group of closest friends , carried with him two cups of coffee that I recognized came from La Casita del Café Colombiano , a chain that was just beginning to be known in the United States. Later I learned that its original owners required that each branch be in the hands of Venezuelans or Colombians of proven reputation. I'll keep an eye on it, I told myself. That was one of the projects I had in mind for the future. Socializing accompanied by a good cup of coffee, or hot chocolate, and a good book, in a place of encounters and reunions.

I took my glass decorated with the drawing of a white Andean house with red tile roofs. The size of the glass seemed to me an exaggerated presentation of how I thought that delicious drink should be served, but at that moment I would have even drank not only mine, but Orlando's as well. Maybe what they wanted to achieve with those big glasses was that you would drink more, and each time you would need more of that drink, like those addicted to anything else.

I wanted answers and explanations. I needed to know.

"Calm down," he said. "I'll tell you everything."

THE MARKED PREY

THE PAPERS

We had finished our coffee. That coffee tasted divine. When he saw that I was more awake and calm, he thought I was ready to receive the news he had for me. Orlando placed a briefcase on the kitchen table. He opened it and took out the first folder. It wasn't the only one. He had everything very well organized.

The first thing was to inform me that I was no longer in Mexico.

"How? What? Then where am ?"

"Alma, you are in the United States. We had to get you out of there without your consent or your knowledge. It was a decision we had to take as an emergency measure, since we had information from very good sources that an attack was being planned against you, a second attack. The first was the one in which you were shot, do you remember?"

"How could I not remember? But I thought it was meant for my husband."

"No, Almita, it was aimed at you, and your husband was behind it all. What happened is that you moved just in time and the bullet ended up grazing your neck."

That news made me tremble.

"You were, and still are, a sure target. You know a lot, perhaps too much, about all the operations of the criminal groups in which Ramiro and the others are involved. It is not in their interest for you to remain alive. The moment we received the information, we decided to proceed with your kidnapping. Look, the news is everywhere."

We turned on the television and looked for the news on the Spanish-language stations. They were interviewing my husband, sad and distressed, almost crying. He asked his wife's kidnappers to contact him. He was willing to pay whatever it took. My photo was in all the newspapers, in all the media.

"We reassured you. We coordinated everything with the authorities of Homeland Security, the DEA and the Ministry of Justice. That's how we brought you here where we have been monitoring you while you slept. Kiana has already gone out for walks with me several times. We will give you your new documents in a few days. We must first change your physical appearance a little."

"My new documents? Change my physical appearance?" I asked. "That's like changing my identity. I'm happy with myself ," I told him.

I didn't feel comfortable with everything that was happening, but Orlando convinced me that there was no other option, unless I wanted to run the risk of being recognized and attacked by the cartels and international mafias, especially the Latin American ones. They were everywhere.

"Right now you are in a safe place. Tomorrow you have an appointment with a plastic surgeon. No, he is not just a plastic surgeon, he is the most renowned for changing identities and they are going to make you even more beautiful than you already are, you will see. So tonight will be the last time you recognize yourself in the mirror. I will accompany you."

Musiú told me that this was done in very important cases. These were necessary risks. You will also have psychological help to help you accept your new identity. Since we have to change your name too, we are going to give you a list of some that we have considered might "suit" you so that you can choose the one you like best. You don't have to tell me now, but you do have to tell me before your appointment with the doctor.

Considering all the possible options, what else was left for me? I felt like I was between a rock and a hard place.

"Okay. I don't really like the idea, but I understand it."

"Try to rest as much as you can. I'll pick you up early tomorrow." He hugged me and left.

THE MIRROR

I thought about it. It would be a bit weird, but I had to do it. It didn't take me long to decide. From now on I would be called Maria Silvia. Maria was the name of my older sister, whom I have admired since I was little. I have always liked the middle name.

Orlando picked me up early. After dropping me off at the clinic, he took care of the little dog, who also needed attention. When I came out of the operating room, I was covered in bandages. I felt like a Christmas mummy. A nurse came every day to change them. I wasn't allowed to look in the mirror yet.

A hairdresser also came. They changed the color of my hair and the style. Seeing myself in the mirror had to wait.

Kiana was still by my side, as always. She was no longer as agile as before and gray hairs were beginning to form around her eyes and muzzle. That's life.

Finally the day of the mirror arrived.

"And who is that?"

I couldn't believe that it was me. I felt really weird. I was and I wasn't, that was the question, like in Shakespeare's Hamlet. Describing myself, for now, was very difficult. It's like when you go to the hairdresser and they cut your hair and leave it completely different from the one you had before, but multiplied to the nth power. In this case, it wasn't just the hair, it was everything! Even the dog looked confused. She shook her head as if she were trying to locate me from a different angle. I petted her. My voice, my caresses and my smell gave her confidence. I told her that everything was going to be okay. I think she began to accept my new style. One gets used to everything. Amen.

There was then a photo shoot for all the official documents. I had been granted citizenship without even having asked for it. It was like a lightning process in exchange for more information. Everything is always in exchange for something.

I was a special protected witness. I was wanted, and my protectors knew it. I was, once again, a key asset.

This time I was the one who wanted to know in detail everything that was behind my kidnapping, my role in the life and death of so many, and the current state of those I had helped. I wanted to know what had happened to those who had managed to continue on their way after being let go from the shelter. All of that would leave traces on me that neither plastic surgery nor therapies could erase.

Orlando told me what he could. That's how I understood it.

But not everything would have answers or explanations. Sometimes it is better not to know them.

Recovering my self-esteem would also be a long process, I was aware of that. I no longer wanted to be the victim, and the key to the prison I had built for myself began to open the bars. I could learn to walk freely, without microphones or bodyguards, without fear. Yes, I felt low on energy and without desire. I didn't feel like continuing like this, without hope, like a robot whose days and nights pass by. Thank God I had my dog who, in a certain way, forced me to get up, to move, to live. Suddenly a song from Venezuela would play somewhere, maybe it was just in my mind, and then my spirit would return, but also my longing. I would sing it at the top of my lungs, and I would dance to it.

Déjà vu. I finally left the suite. Orlando took us to a place that looked like a normal house, a simple house. As I entered, I went into a room where a group of people trained in interrogation would ask me the questions they had prepared and written in front of them. They would take turns, ask me for more details, and let me rest and walk around from time to time. Musiú would only be a witness and would not intervene.

As I answered the questions, I relived everything almost as if it were live and direct, like the flashbacks that I had frequently, day and night, and that I was trying to control with the help of the therapies. I cried while answering some, I screamed with rage while answering others. I trembled with fear and anguish. At night I woke up screaming, thinking that I was escaping from criminals who threatened to slit my throat like they had done with

Mariela. It was a matter of time and hard work. The PTSD, also known as post-traumatic stress disorder, that I had been diagnosed with could improve. They would continue to help me until I could live an independent life without surprises.

That interrogation lasted more than eight hours. It would be the only one, and the last one, according to them, although I would have to be available to identify some subjects if necessary. I felt exhausted, depressed and exhausted, both physically and mentally. These interrogations were extremely hard.

THE NEW PLAN

From that moment on, I had to accept what had been programmed for me. The ultimate goal was to give me back the peace and freedom I had lost. The passionate and almost blind energy of helping everyone who needed it would no longer be so passionate, nor so blind. I would be more selective with my priorities. I would learn that you shouldn't say yes to everything.

For now, I was given a nearly new house, fully furnished and fenced, in a well-to-do middle-class neighborhood. The community also had a 24-hour gated entrance, and no one was allowed in without permission. The house also had cameras and alarms everywhere. The backyard had fruit trees and lots of flowers. Kiana had a nice space, and she dedicated herself not only to walking around and leaving her mark, but also to making holes with her front paws. I could never take that skill away from her. Now I would use her help to plant bushes and flowers in those holes. Thanks, Kiana.

In the garage, there was a late-model car. It was a hybrid pickup truck, military green in color, with four-wheel drive, very powerful and comfortable. Of course, it was armored.

My first big obstacle was English. It was essential. I understood the need to study it. The people, those who had brought me here, had been very clear. I had no doubt about the effort it would take to understand and speak it. I was willing to do whatever work was necessary. When you are a little older it is quite an uphill battle. The sounds are different, the same words can mean opposite things. For me it was a difficult language to understand and speak. I kept an open mind. There are sounds, however, that are difficult to pronounce. The combination of T and H is an example. Also the mixture of vowels, and depending on whether they are at the beginning, at the end or in the middle of words, and what other letters they are accompanied by, they are complicated, and we often get into trouble because we want to say something and something different comes out. When I see that I have made a mistake I see on the face of the person who is listening to me that expression of not having understood well. I laugh, they laugh, and I correct the spelling of what I want to say. There are sounds that are difficult to pronounce. The combination of the "t" and the "h" sounds like our "z." Also the mixture of the vowels, if they are at the beginning, at the end or in the middle of the words and what other letters they are accompanied by is a bit complicated, and I often get into trouble when I want to say something and I said something else. The moment I see the face of the person who is listening to me I realize that I have made a mistake. I laugh, they laugh, and I correct the mistake.

I had been enrolled in my first intensive course. Eight hours a day, Monday to Friday. I was advised to only watch films in English, to watch the news, and to repeat everything I could and however I could, even if I didn't understand anything, as if I were an echo, a copy. The English school was quite strict and demanding, and every week we had to learn a song by heart. I'm very bad at singing. I've been very out of tune all my life. In the school choir they even asked me to open my mouth as if I were singing, but without making any sounds. Yes, I'm that bad. I think the genes and the gift for music were shared among my sisters before I was born, my simple conclusion. I accept.

They also gave us classes on American culture, the country's customs, how we should behave, food, history and politics, the constitution, paying taxes, and the discrimination between whites and blacks. That was something I had never experienced before in our countries, where the color of your skin is not what identifies you as better or worse. In short, it was a fairly complete program.

On weekends, I had a therapist who specialized in major trauma visit me. She helped me a lot. Also, Orlando came on Sundays and accompanied me on walking the dog on some trails off the property. There, Kiana ran around without limitations. She didn't go far and came back as soon as we mentioned her name.

Orlando was the only thing familiar in this new stage of my life, the only thing I had known before, my only friend. With him I vented my anguish and stress. "The world is wide and foreign," he told me one day. He left those words hanging in the air, without further explanation.

On Sundays, after Musiú's visit and the walk with Kiana, I took the rest of the afternoon to go to the gym. There I started to make some friends, the same ones who went every Sunday, like me. Socially, I didn't want anyone to notice me. It's not that I wasn't excited to have a special friend-partner, but I was still married to Ramiro and I couldn't make room for that kind of relationship. That door was completely closed.

My neighbors were all English-speaking. I couldn't escape this much-needed cultural immersion. At first I didn't speak to anyone, but I couldn't continue like that either. The first six or seven months, or maybe more, were almost torture for me. I felt like I didn't belong, I felt so isolated, so different from everyone else. I felt like the people on the street, like the "homeless," although I did have one, on loan. Yes, I had a house, but I didn't have a home. I needed to share "with desire," with others.

THE UNEXPECTED NEWS

Again, another change.
They moved us to the north.
More instructions, more checks, more surprises. The most unexpected was Musiú's farewell. He was transferred to Colombia where he would be responsible for monitoring the borders with Venezuela and Panama. He promised me that he would continue to keep an eye on me.

In reality, I did not want to remain in the United States, nor did I want to depend on Orlando for everything. The DEA needed me and protected me. I knew firsthand the protagonists of the underworld of drug trafficking and all kinds of human and organ smuggling that grew and interconnected internationally with leaders, cartels and financial entities. The business of the century, unregistered, with millions in profits that were not declared and not taxed. Money laundering, now openly, dominated the economy of some of the countries involved. Tax havens were very useful, as were some banks that kept accounts secret or used the names of some front men to protect those deposits, private islands converted into 'confidential' sexual havens that offered the services of young girls and migrant girls to people in power, in short, the list is endless.

Not only had I seen and experienced first-hand how human beings have deteriorated so much, but now I was seeing the same thing again, the game with trading chips, each one with the faces of immigrants, with their lives, in a first world society. It didn't only happen on this continent. I read the news coming from Europe and the cases were similar. There, however, some agents of certain mafias related to the abuse of migrants had been brought to justice.

TRAPPED WITH NO WAY OUT

That's how I was beginning to feel. Manipulated with the illusion of being free in the most controlled country in the world.

In reality, I would never have thought of leaving Venezuela, but things happened as fate had written for me. Without a doubt, I felt grateful for so much and for everything.

The organization sent me far away, almost as far as the North Pole. Washington State, right next to Canada. That place was a pretty safe place for me. That's where I went with Kiana. I needed to stabilize myself, to connect, to get involved, to belong in some way. I had too much pent-up energy and I needed to use it for productive things.

Again, I was placed in a very nice little house, in the middle of nowhere and surrounded by nature. My closest neighbors were about a half mile away, so I rarely saw them. They were letting go of the reins a bit and I took advantage of the opportunity to start planting myself, like the trees. It is very difficult for the body and mind to be changing location so frequently.

I was already doing pretty well with English, although you always carry the accent of someone who learns the language "from old age." Every time

I opened my mouth, the first thing I heard was... oh, you have an accent. Where are you from? At first I would answer with one or two words, and that was it. I felt embarrassed to talk. After a while I told myself that I had to change my attitude. I had to use my accent as a tool to break the ice, to be able to be part of the community. That change was very positive in every way. Personally, it helped me with my self-esteem; I was no longer afraid to speak with an accent.

I opened the doors to apply for and accept some simple jobs. I was starting to test my surroundings. No, I couldn't work as a veterinarian. That happens when we come to another country. We were used to being somebody, and here we start from scratch. Discipline and a lot of effort are required to get ahead. I had to accept that reality with much sadness, but I went back to college and learned many other things that would help me feel useful again. I enrolled in Law School. I thought I could be useful again with a new degree under my arm, and I also liked it quite a bit. I would defend those in need.

Little by little, I started getting invited to birthday parties so different. There was a time to arrive and a time to leave. People seemed boring to me, they didn't dance, they didn't sing, but they did tell jokes that I didn't find funny at all. So you pretend and smile. And nobody stays after the stipulated time. But why isn't it a party?

THE IMMIGRANT'S MANUAL

Just as there are no manuals for being a parent, there are no manuals for learning how to be an immigrant. Those that are out there are a kind of guide with suggestions. Each case is very particular, and so is each country. "When in Rome, do as the Romans do" is the best advice.

I would add that it is very important not to compare cultures. We always think that ours, the one from our land, is the best. And yes, it is the best because we get used to it, but we have to learn from the others, from here and from there. Everything we learn and experience enriches us, just as we also enrich the cultures of others. Let's celebrate our differences.

It was so cold. My first real winter. It had already snowed. It was an indescribable thrill to see those snowflakes falling all over. The landscape was white, silent, beautiful, peaceful. Kiana and I went out to play. She loved it and so did I. It was incredible. It was such a thrill. I pinched the snow to see if it was real. It melted between my fingers covered in warm gloves, maybe it was melting from the heat of my hands. I made a snowman like I had seen in the movies. I put a cap on it with the colors of the Venezuelan flag. I thought it would be easier to do it, but even with my thick gloves, my hands were freezing. I took pictures and posted them on Facebook.

The next day the snowman was still intact. It was frozen. I felt proud of my creation.

The snow didn't last long. The days dawned with very low temperatures. As we got up early and went out for a walk, still in the dark, we used a flashlight that lit the path with little ice stars as we walked. The crunch of dry leaves sounded under my boots. The branches of the bare trees were also covered with frozen droplets, like natural Christmas decorations. We couldn't walk very far because the pads of the dog's toes froze, and she refused to wear her boots. She would shake them off as soon as she put them on and she never liked them. When I came home I would protect her little paws with Vaseline. She seemed to like this "winter pedicure" treatment.

A FEW MONTHS HAVE PASSED

After many months without seeing him, Orlando came to visit us. He was the only familiar face I had seen after so long. He arrived without warning. When I saw him, tears came to my eyes. They were tears of emotion, of joy. I threw myself into his arms. That contact was very significant, and I missed it. Did I miss him, or the hug?

Here people don't hug each other, they stay at arm's length. I feel it as a rejection of the unknown, I told him.

"Yes, I know. We will always be different," he replied.

"Come on, let's sit here. Let me order a pizza. Would you like that? I remember you really liked the margarita with anchovies and black olives."

"Good memory. That's right."

He called the only pizzeria in town that delivered. It would arrive in about half an hour.

As we were setting the table, I walked into the living room to grab the remote to turn off the television. Before I could do so, I looked back at the set. Breaking news was on.

"Orlando, Orlando," I called him. "Look what they're saying. They just captured Ramiro in Michoacán and they're processing his extradition to the United States. They accuse him of a lot of things, from homicides to smuggling weapons, people, organs, and drug trafficking. There was a big reward on his head. It was his beloved cousin Rafael who tipped off his whereabouts. There, in what had been our mansion, they caught him and he didn't put up any resistance. They also searched the entire house and took a number of boxes with documents, photographs, plans and maps, plans and reports. I think they got more than they were looking for from some of the information I had shared about the hiding places."

However, with so much money involved and so much corruption, the Mexican authorities would have been able to ignore it. I left the television on to continue listening to the details.

Said and done. A shootout had broken out between the police and the National Guard and the Michoacán Cartel, which was better armed, another of Ramiro's illegal businesses. He had contacts with a camouflaged distributor of war weapons from the United States. The final result was the death of 9 policemen, and my husband was rescued and hidden. Rafael, for his part, fled Mexico to Venezuela, where his contacts would protect him.

I was shaking.

"Calm down, Alma."

"I'm not Alma anymore, I'm María Silvia," I told him.

"To me you are still Alma. Your heart is still the same."

There was a knock at the door. It was the guy with the still-warm pizzas. That was what the ads guaranteed. Sure, the pizzas arrived quickly. There was no traffic. Orlando paid for them and we sat down at the table.

We had dinner.

This time the pizza I liked so much tasted like cardboard. I was only able to eat one slice. The rest was swallowed by the dog.

"Thank goodness you're here now," I said to Musiú. My head was spinning. I was beginning to relive my past again.

"What will happen now?"

"I don't know," he replied, "but I can imagine that they will call you back to testify if they manage to catch him."

"Ramiro has not stopped looking for you and has private detectives everywhere. He does not forgive you for abandoning him. He also does not forgive you for leaving the DNA results of Lupe's baby on the nightstand and for sending a copy to the local newspapers. The scandal had been huge. He had been asked to resign, but he continued to cling to power. Many people would lose their businesses if my still husband resigned from his position. He pursued and ordered the murder of some of the journalists who had published the story".

"And what happened to Guadalupe and her little son?" I asked.

"They went into hiding in Father José's church. From there they were taken to Mexico City. The Apostolic Nunciature facilitated their departure to the Vatican, where she would help in the kitchen. Her little son was given, or rather, sold "for adoption" to an influential French couple who paid a good amount of money for him."

TOTAL PARANOIA

Never underestimate your enemies.

How could I do that?

Since Orlando told me that there were detectives looking for me, I began to feel like I was being followed at all times.

The town had two Mexican restaurants, both excellent. I went there frequently to eat and had become friends with the owners. If I needed to find someone to do work around the house, I looked for references, and I had always been referred to hard-working people.

One day I went to ask if they knew any good bricklayers. I asked in both places and they all gave me the same name. A bricklayer who had just arrived from Michoacán. What were the chances? It was the same Raúl who had been doing work for us at the mansion.

I hired him to do some repairs around the house.

When he arrived we talked about what he had in mind.

He didn't recognize me, but he did recognize the dog. He told me that the dog looked a lot like Doña Santa, the governor's wife.

"It's exactly the same, boss."

I told him that it couldn't be possible, that maybe it looked like his, but mine was from here.

I played dumb. I knew he suspected me.

I asked him to come back "tomorrow," although for us Latinos that word can simply mean "in the future." I explained that it was tomorrow, Tuesday morning, when I would expect him.

So, Raul came out. I think I saw him taking pictures with his cell phone.

I immediately called Orlando and told him what had happened.

He promised me that tomorrow morning, when Raul arrived, he would have a security team outside. He also gave me a microphone that would record everything I said to the worker, and they would act if necessary.

Raul arrived in his truck, with a trailer full of construction materials. He rang the doorbell. I opened it. He went into the house without any problems.

We started talking about work, and suddenly he pulled a big gun out of the back of his belt. He pointed it at me and said: "Lady Santa, did you think I wouldn't recognize you?"

The special group immediately came in, handcuffed him and took him away. They also took me and the dog to another safe house. We were no longer safe. The hitman had copies of my documents with the new identity that Raúl was able to steal from one of the kitchen drawers while I had left to go to the bathroom.

Once again I had to disappear. Could it ever end?

DON'T EVEN THINK ABOUT IT

There are things that are non-negotiable for me, I replied to the officer who was trying to convince me that I had to get rid of Kiana. Kiana was like an extension of myself, I would never separate myself from her, even if it put my life at risk. My dog had dedicated her whole life to me. The least I could do for her was to take care of her in her final years.

Now we were in a bunker with all the comforts, but without windows. Once again, prisoners, and without having been accused or tried.

I was bored, even though a fitness trainer helped me stay active and I had an excellent library and a balanced menu prepared by a nutritionist and a group of trusted cooks. However, the food was tested and approved before it was sent to me.

I also made the most of the library. I followed the Law School program that I had already started. I studied all the subjects with dedication. I asked for the books I needed, and they brought them to me. I used cards where I wrote data about dates, names and places, history, trials. I memorized almost the entire Constitution. I also asked for the Master's program in Immigration. My small part would help humanize it. And I managed to graduate with honors, in captivity.

During those days I devoted myself to writing. It helped me to maintain my sanity, to remember and to give my opinions. I let off steam with words. It had become my new project and little by little it became a discipline that absorbed me. The scenes, both familiar and invented, passed before my mind as if it were a movie. It was something strange and difficult to describe, but I lived it with passion.

Every two hours I would get up. I would stretch, read, study, play with my dog for a while, and turn on the television. I loved watching real-life documentaries, world travel, and some game shows. I also loved the news, which was rarely good.

Today, a news item broke my heart. A young man from my homeland had murdered a nursing student. I felt so ashamed, as if I were an outsider! Similar cases of rape and robbery perpetrated by my undocumented countrymen were becoming daily horror stories. An irrational reason behind the new and exacerbated feeling of xenophobia, especially against the "latest generation Venezuelans," born and raised under dictatorial regimes. What they have learned from their leaders is violence, crime, abuse and lies, injustice. There is no forgiveness for so much harm, in my beloved Venezuela, as now, spreading throughout the world.

We pay together for sinners, and it is not fair.

I would begin to prepare a campaign to clear my country's name. Again, from my imposed secrecy, I began to design a strategy. A small team of volunteers would receive my plan in writing, although they would not know where I was.

First, we would denounce those who were tarnishing our honor, including murderers and thieves, as well as corrupt professionals who had stolen our heritage and now lived like celebrities. We would obtain evidence to unmask them and make them pay. Utopia? Nothing seemed impossible to me anymore. For now it was just a thought.

KIANA

Yesterday she turned 14. I had decided that her birth date was the day I received her in front of my clinic, even though she was not a newborn. I still had the card that came with her.

Except for the years we lived in Mexico, since we left there Kiana had gotten used to sleeping in bed with me, but she wouldn't get on until she noticed I was completely asleep. Then, without making any noise, she would slowly climb on. I would notice her after a few hours when it was my turn to change position and I would find resistance. It was her, lying next to me. I didn't want to wake her up and my stretching had to be limited. My side of the bed was much narrower than hers. We both snored.

Today, when I turned around, I found her different.

She had passed away without asking my permission. She knew I wouldn't give it to her. I cried for days. Inconsolable. My faithful companion had gone, the one who had gone through good times and bad with me without complaining, without protesting. She never demanded anything from me or judged me, and always seemed to be happy when she was by my side.

I felt her passing as much as I celebrated her life and the privilege of having accompanied her and lived with her. I mourned her as I had never mourned before. Losing her was like losing myself.

COULD I COME OUT OF MY HIDING PLACE NOW?

It was time to face the situation again. I was tired of living like an earthworm, below the surface.

I would remain as one more in the crowd.

But I wasn't just one more.

I went to the College of Physics, whose programs I had completed from the bunker. I made an appointment with the dean. I told him part of my story, why I was semi-hidden, and explained that I wanted to practice as an immigration lawyer, and eventually become a judge. The dean looked at me with curiosity, to use a more or less acceptable word. I asked to be examined under special conditions, so that I could pass the final test to be officially accepted as a jurist. He promised to contact me after he consulted the Faculty Council.

His call came.

He told me that in this unique and very special case, I would be allowed to take an oral exam in front of a panel of five judges.

The date of the big moment has arrived.

Yes, I was nervous but confident.

I went into the exam room, which lasted a few hours. They would record it with my permission to review it before delivering their verdict. I had spoken every word with the awareness that I was giving the best of my legal and immigration knowledge. Now it was in the hands of God and the judges.

The days passed slowly and the answer did not arrive.
I was losing hope.
I refused to think of a Plan B, in case this one didn't work.
Orlando, almost as loyal as Kiana, came to visit again. He was always very attentive to me.
I was having breakfast with him at home when he handed me a small box that he took out of his pocket. He opened it. Inside was a simple, beautiful ring. He wanted to get engaged to me. He told me that he had bought the ring the week we met at that conference in Mexico. This man has been very patient, I thought. I should get a divorce and I could do it now. It had been more than the required time to ask for it from a distance, and with enough reasons for it to be granted. I said YES. We were both super happy. We had been through the good and the bad together. He also told me that he had been the one who had left Kiana for me on my birthday. And yes, his handwriting was the same.
We began our procedures with haste. We did not want to wait another day.
After three months, I received a sealed envelope which I had to confirm receipt with my signature. I signed it and opened it.

A letter of congratulations signed by the Dean and the entire Faculty of Law Council stated that I had been awarded the title of lawyer and Immigration Judge. There was no precedent for such decisions. I had passed all the exams with the highest marks.

Not only did I have the degree, but I was also offered the Chair to teach, since I not only knew about the legal implications of asylum and immigration processes, but I had also lived and experienced them.

My joys had multiplied. Musiú was also very proud of me.

Meanwhile, Orlando was nominated for the Senate by the Independent Party, and to everyone's surprise, since he was not a member of either of the two major parties in this country, he won his seat.

A few months passed.

My divorce was a reality. The posters posted seeking Ramiro's signature were never answered, so I was granted the divorce on the grounds of abandonment and lack of opposition. I felt as if the weight of rocks I had carried on my back for so many years had crumbled into sand that filtered through and became part of the world. It is difficult to describe that feeling of freedom.

That night we went out to celebrate all the good vibes that were coming our way. We went to one of the best Italian restaurants in Georgetown where we began to plan our near future. Georgetown is a historic district in Washington DC. For me, it was a magical, spectacular place. After so much time studying alone, and before challenging the university authorities with the idea of recognition of my learning, I had spent countless hours in the District Public Library. Libraries had a special meaning for me. In my homeland they practically do not exist, except for the National Library in Caracas that had been created in 1883. I went there many times. The smell of books, the honor of being present before the wisdom behind so many publications was for me something almost unreal. I felt like I had been transported to another galaxy where I could give free rein to my imagination. Here, unlike there, the libraries are extraordinary, with a network system that interconnects them and finds almost any book you request. In addition, they organize presentations and many other meetings for the benefit of the community, and they are free, accessible to everyone. In short, they are wonderful.

At the restaurant we sat at a small table away from the crowd, very romantic. A red candle lit in front of us and a small vase with orange and yellow roses decorated our corner. Dinner was served to us. Antipasto to start, risotto that we shared, and tiramisu for dessert. We drank a few glasses of the house red wine. A delicious dinner, an exclusive, yet cozy atmosphere.

Orlando and I dressed up nicely, it was a very special occasion.

"So, are we getting married?"

"Of course, my love," I told him excitedly. We both could and wanted to. We had waited so long, so long. The details: A very intimate and simple ceremony. Us, the judge, and a group of close friends.

The ceremony, unique, very much ours.

We also decided that we would live in Georgetown, one of my favorite places. Convenient for Musiú, my husband, since it was relatively close to the Capitol, and also for me, who had set up an office to provide legal aid to immigrants, and where the Court where I would work as an Immigration Judge was also located.

MY FIRST CASE

As they say, a crab is a difficult and complicated case. It would be like a test of fire for me.

A family seeking political asylum came to me. The father, Alberto Gomez, a young man of about 35, was light-skinned and of medium height. He looked strong. He did not seem to have been going through the hardship that other immigrants experienced. His wife, a little younger than him, also had olive-brown skin and long black hair tied back in a braid, and two children, five and seven years old. Their lawyer told me their story. They had left Venezuela, like so many others, and had arrived in Texas. From there, from the immigration detention center, they had been transferred here. The testimony they presented to me was very similar to that of so many I had interviewed when I lived in Michoacán, but there was "something" that did not fit. I did not know what it was, yet, and I would not make a decision lightly.

I made an appointment with them in three days.

I went to my office and called my assistant, a very clever paralegal with a lot of energy.

Look, Gabriela, I told her. I want you to find out something for me. I want you to go to the Department of Justice very early tomorrow morning to verify this information (I gave her an envelope with a copy of the passports and the asylum application) and, in addition, to compare the fingerprints of this family with the files they have there. I am going to send an official written communication from this court to Roberto García so that he can speed up the process and give you the results, if possible, tomorrow itself. I had already called him by phone, but a written record is required in these cases. There was no time to lose.

At the same time, I ordered the names and whereabouts of those who had crossed the border with Mr. Gomez and his family to be determined. They, the Gomezes, would be held at the local center while their application was approved.

Three days later they returned to court with their lawyer.

I decided to question them in my office, one by one, even the children. The lawyer would be present with each one of them. We would record everything with their permission.

The questions would be similar to those asked of all other asylum seekers. The answers, in the case of this particular family, seemed to have been memorized, the same as Alberto and the rest. Uhmmmm, too perfect and convincing. Unfortunately for them, they had fallen into my court.

Again I asked them to come back the following week.

I listened to the recordings over and over again. Something strange, something very strange. For being Venezuelans, according to them, having lived there all their lives, they had been left blank by some of the questions I had asked them, using very typical expressions of ours. They acted like they hadn't heard the questions correctly. Both Alberto and Yajaira had made a big mistake, but not the little children who, as we were able to verify, had indeed been born in Venezuela.

Roberto Garcia came to my office in person. He brought with him a detailed report of what he had achieved.

"The fingerprints and passports, Your Honor, are genuine, but..."

"But what?" I asked.

The fingerprints match those found in the International Fingerprint Bank, and belong to a couple of Iranian origin. This is a network of terrorists from Iran who arrived in Venezuela, where they continued their training, not only in military practices but also in learning Spanish with a Venezuelan accent. For this purpose they had been in a Center created for this purpose in Maracaibo, Zulia State.

Once they successfully passed their language and culture exams, they were given passports made in Cuba, which implied that they were Venezuelan by birth, and thus they would enter the United States as immigrants seeking asylum for humanitarian reasons. This couple had already undergone nine years of intensive training, during which they were urged to have children to appear more real. So the little ones were indeed nationals.

That case opened a Pandora's box that would have alarming consequences internationally.

PRUDENT SOUL

"My love, remember these two words, prudence and patience. You are facing a reality that could lead us to an international conflict. Orlando had an inkling of what was going on, as he had been involved in many investigations before becoming a Senator in the Congress of the United States. For my part, I felt that what I had before me was much more serious than I could have imagined."

"Remember, darling, one false step and..."

"And?"

"Now we were faced with a struggle between political powers, which, once again, used immigrants as shields, as pawns. It was a silent war between East and West for the conquest of the world, the control of the new order. To do this, countries made alliances to overthrow the most powerful. All against one was the slogan. Little by little, they invaded the United States secretly, silently, with capable immigrants passing through who destabilized the peace to open the way for enemy powers. That is why they came to ask for asylum with the excuse of being persecuted."

"In this way, they fooled many authorities, and a fairly large number of these false subjects had already entered and obtained their asylums. In the case of Alberto and Yajaira, I would have to use my wisdom and my contacts, and at the same time, I could not prove that I knew what they also knew.

When they came to my courtroom to hear my decision, they were asked to leave their phones outside, including the phone number of the lawyer representing them. While I distracted them by explaining their obligations and responsibilities, their rights and duties as asylum seekers, and the restrictions that they could not leave the country for a period of 5 years, my agents reviewed the content of their phones. In addition to that, they installed special chips to listen to their conversations and locate them geographically. I gained time while I waited for them to send me a signal from outside that everything was ready to finish signing the papers that we had marked with a special ink that would give them away at the right moment.

They thanked me profusely. They had found what they were looking for. I wasn't so sure.

My court was always packed with cases to be resolved. There were only a few judges for so many applications. I began to meet defense attorneys who charged a fortune for their services, who promised their clients that everything would be resolved in a short time, and kept their hopes high. Some of these professionals invented novels of love and pain in order to win their cases, and even presented overwhelming and hard-to-believe evidence to support asylum applications. I was already getting to know them. Without any scruples or prejudices, they took advantage of ignorance and the great need to escape poverty by flaying the little that migrants had left. Not all of them were corrupt, but there was a considerable number of them. My court also began to keep notes of these individuals.

THANKSGIVING WAS APPROACHING

Although it is not our custom to celebrate this day, I have always liked it for everything it implies; the welcome given to the first pilgrims who arrived at this place by the indigenous people with whom they shared the fruits of their harvests and the blessings for having arrived at these holy lands. Time has transformed the background of this celebration, but it is still preserved as an opportunity for families to get together to celebrate.

This year we decided to start a tradition in our house.

Of the cases that I had attended during that year, I would invite two families to come and share that day with us.

This year we invited a family from Sudan. Mariam had arrived with three children through an organization that helped refugees. Her husband had been killed, as had a large number of young men, leaving the women widowed, without support and without resources.

The other family that came was originally from the Philippines. Jose (no accent on the é) had arrived in the United States when he was a boy of 8 years old. His mother had sent him with a coyote, who had been paid with all of her savings from hard, low-paying work. She thought she wanted a better future for her son. Here his grandparents would receive him. Undocumented for many years, and unable to return to Manila, he was stuck here. When DACA, a program that was created to help all children brought without identity papers by their parents as a door to the path to obtaining a permanent permit to stay in the United States, Jose no longer qualified. There was an age limit to be considered. He had a birthday just a few months before the deadline, and was no longer eligible.

So Mariam, her three children, Jose and his grandmother Lala, and we spent a very pleasant evening. Mariam was already an asylum seeker and had found work in a family home that allowed her to live with her children in an annex. The children were already going to school and were slowly adapting to American life, so different from that of Sudan. We arranged for Jose to get an exceptional permit so that he would no longer have to hide from the authorities. My husband hired him as the press chief for his office in the Senate, since Jose was able to graduate as a journalist.

We also invited Gabriela, one of my assistants. Her family lived in Wisconsin and she would be alone this year.

After that celebration we invented other ones, birthdays, good grades at school, anything would be a good reason to celebrate. That little group became inseparable and helped each other. Jose and Gabriela also became more than inseparable.

Not everything ended badly for everyone.

MORE CASES WERE OPENED

Investigations into terrorist groups continued. All cases were documented and the "asylum seekers" located. They lived in close neighborhoods. All their steps were followed. That was now in the hands of the Department of Justice, Homeland Security and Defense.

The corrupt lawyers were brought before the Senate Ethics Committee. Their licenses were revoked and they were prosecuted and imprisoned for their crimes.

Many migrants, unfortunately, have learned to use and abuse the system for their own benefit, causing distrust among the American people who have opened the doors of their homes to them.

After many years of solving so much in our lives, Orlando and I decided it was time to retire. We were satisfied with everything we had done to contribute to humanity.

We have left a legacy, a mark of our passage through this land. We had given our lives, our souls and our hearts, to defend what seemed indefensible, sometimes risking ourselves without measuring the danger. We have no regrets.

Our years were already many, and we had few left. We would take advantage of it while our bodies allowed us.

Mariam stayed at our house and we went off to travel the world. A reward well-earned and well deserved.

There will always be good and evil, like two sides of a coin that look in opposite directions but cannot be separated from each other.

THE END

REFERENCE

It is important to support and sustain this novel with proven facts that can illuminate the consciences and paths of those who read it.

For me, migration means voluntary or forced movement, of humans and animals, with the common goal of improving.
https://www.significados.com/migracion/

1. U.S. Immigration Laws are constantly changing.
   https://www.uscis.gov/laws-and-policies/legislation/immigration-and-nationality-law
2. Undocumented immigrants in the United States contribute significantly to the tax system. In 2022, they paid $96.7 billion in federal, state, and local taxes. Although they do not have work authorization rights, their financial impact is notable.
   https://elplaneta.com/2024/08/02/immigration/undocumented-immigrants-contribute-almost-100000-million-in-taxes-per-year-in-the-usa/
3. Many migrants die or disappear without a trace
   https://www.migrationdataportal.org/en/themes/migrant-deaths-and-disappearances
4. The kidney mafia is known all over the world
   https://www.biobiochile.cl/noticias/sociedad/debate/2023/10/07/impact-in-pakistan-mafia-trafficking-more-than-300-human-kidneys-for-illegal-

      transplants-in-the-world.shtml
      https://www.lapatilla.com/2022/04/26/venta-rinones-trafico-organos-venezuela/
5. Asylum for sale, big business
https://blog.pmpress.org/2023/01/06/asylum-for-sale-but-at-what-cost/
6. Who defends migrants? Do they have rights?
https://www.migrationdataportal.org/en/themes/migrant-rights
7. What other factors influence the migration process?
https://grupoigneo.com/blog/humanizar-la-migracion-una-tarea-pendiente/
https://www.amazon.com/Humanizing-Immigration-Transform-Racist-Unjust/dp/0807008028
8. Deportation
http://humanizandoladeportacion.ucdavis.edu/es/2024/06/27/431-una-migracion-inteligente/
https://www.usa.gov/es/deportacion-estados-unidos
https://es.euronews.com/my-europe/2024/10/07/17-european-paises-demand-un-cambio-de-paradigma-para-deportar-a-los-solicitantes-de-asilo-
9. Refugee camps or concentration camps
https://eacnur.org/en/news/displaced-persons/world-map-displacements-refugees
10. Modern slavery and its relationship with migration processes
https://ourrescue.org/en/education/research-and-trends/modern-slavery-an-invisible-epidemic-in-plain-sight

MAP OF CRIMES USING ARTIFICIAL INTELLIGENCE

LITERATURE

HING, Bill Ong. Humanizing Immigrations. How to transform our racist and unjust system. Beacon Press, 2023

HIRSI ALI, Ayaan. Nomad. From Islam to America. A personal journey through the Clash of civilizations. Free Press, 2010

McGUIRK, Shioban, PINE, Adrienne. Asylum for Sale. Profit and protest in the immigration industry. Kairos, PM Press, 2020

OKRENT, Daniel. The Guarded Gate. Bigotry, eugenics and the law that kept two generations of Jews, Italians and other European immigrants out of America. Scribner, 2019

VARGAS, José Antonio. Dear America, Notes of an Undocumented Citizen. HarperCollins Books, 2018

ZAMORA, Javier. Alone. Penguin Random House Publishing Group, 2022

ACKNOWLEDGEMENTS

To my life partner, accomplice and co-author of this work, Helena Paneyko, for her dedication, her patience and her empathy.

To Heidi Hansen, our editor, for her advice, her creativity, and her contribution to making the dream of publishing our work a reality.

To all those who in one way or another have enriched this novel with their ideas and suggestions

ABOUT THE AUTHOR

Helena Paneyko Mendizábal is the result of the combination of nationalities and cultures, experiences and environments that have enriched her passion for life and her constant tenacity in the face of challenges. In Venezuela she was born, grew up, graduated as a veterinarian, was a congresswoman, had her own radio program, a veterinary hospital, and also wrote weekly for the *Estampas Magazine*, of national circulation. She immigrated to the United States in 1997 with her two children, Alejandro and Daniela. She continued her studies by obtaining a Master's Degree in Education, Leadership and Administration and currently is pursuing a Master's Degree in Creative Writing at the University of Salamanca. In 2015 she made the Camino de Santiago de Compostela alone, traveling along the coast of Portugal, a pilgrimage full of rewarding adventures. She has also lived in Spain and Ireland.

As a writer she has received important recognition. Her contributions have been published, among others, in *Antología de Poemas*, *Tall and True tales of the Olympic Peninsula*, *In the Words of Olympic Peninsula Authors*.

She has successfully published several books, including *Half and Half, Possible, Secrets of Confession, Lost Children of the Vatican,* and *Puro Cuento*.

"I'm not a professional writer," she said, "but when something or someone inspires me, my fingers start dancing on the keyboard to the sound of the music emanating from within me. This is my humble tribute to the universe that adopted me. Based on my reality and a vast imagination, my soul is shamelessly bared in each of the grateful words for so much and for everything."

OTHER BOOKS BY THE AUTHOR

Secretos de Confesión: The story of a family shaped by cultural and beliefs, tangled by discoveries and blackmailing where nothing is secret anymore.

Half and Half: An engaging collection of short stories reflecting the author's experiences in Ireland, Spain, Venezuela and the United States. Readers will be inspired by the El Camino de Santiago pilgrimage. Some stories are in English and some in Spanish. Immerse yourself in adventures that weave many cultural, spiritual, and philosophical perspectives.

Lost Children of the Vatican: It is the story of an extraordinary family inextricably linked to religion's "open secrets." These are things everyone knows but nobody dares to speak about. Reality, intrigue, and romance enliven this novella that will delight readers and awaken their conscience.

IM-Posible: With this work Helena ratifies her literary sensibility, capable of taking us to a world drawn by a fantasy that crystallizes as real in the face of her impressive and unsurpassed style. Helena has earned a worthy place on the threshold of simple and direct literature, awakening in the reader the desire to devour her short stories and poems, without intervals or pauses. It is a book that vanishes in hours of pleasant reading and when we finish it, it leaves us with an exquisite flavor that incites us to wait for the next one. —Robert and Siomi Alonso, Miami, FL

Puro Cuento: A collection of short stories covering humor, satire, imagination, experiences, metaphors and much more.

ABOUT THE TRANSLATOR

Keith Guerin is a writer, first author of an international technical publication and contributing author of technical articles and of college course materials.

A college educated world traveler, both personally and professionally, visiting many countries and experiencing cultures around the world.

Studied languages, Spanish, English, French, and German.

Currently studying ancient history

And finally, a retired professional.

Made in the USA
Monee, IL
08 February 2025